THIS ONE TIME
WITH JULIA

THIS ONE TIME
WITH JULIA

DAVID LAMPSON

An Imprint of Penguin Group (USA) Inc.

This One Time with Julia

RAZORBILL

Published by the Penguin Group

Penguin Young Readers Group

345 Hudson Street, New York, New York 10014, U.S.A.

Penguin Group (USA) Inc., 375 Hudson Street, New York, New York 10014, U.S.A.

Penguin Group (Canada), 90 Eglinton Avenue East, Suite 700, Toronto, Ontario, Canada M4P 2Y3 (a division of Pearson Penguin Canada Inc.)

Penguin Books Ltd, 80 Strand, London WC2R 0RL, England

Penguin Ireland, 25 St Stephen's Green, Dublin 2, Ireland (a division of Penguin Books Ltd)

Penguin Group (Australia), 250 Camberwell Road, Camberwell, Victoria 3124, Australia (a division of Pearson Australia Group Pty Ltd)

Penguin Books India Pvt Ltd, 11 Community Centre, Panchsheel Park, New Delhi – 110 017, India

Penguin Group (NZ), 67 Apollo Drive, Mairangi Bay, Auckland 1311, New Zealand (a division of Pearson New Zealand Ltd)

Penguin Books (South Africa) (Pty) Ltd, 24 Sturdee Avenue, Rosebank, Johannesburg 2196, South Africa

Penguin Books Ltd, Registered Offices: 80 Strand, London WC2R 0RL, England

10 9 8 7 6 5 4 3 2 1

ISBN 978-1-59514-340-2

Library of Congress Cataloging-in-Publication Data is available

Printed in the United States of America

CHAPTER ONE

Back when we were just tiny little kids, Alvin used to make me switch names with him every few weeks. I can't remember when we started doing it, so I might have been born as Alvin for all I know. We weren't identical twins, but we both had light hair and green eyes, and I guess we looked close enough back then, because only our mother seemed to notice when we changed into each other. Around third grade our hair turned dark brown, but my eyes did too, and I started getting a lot bigger than Alvin was, and he told me he was bored of switching names. I happened to be Joe at the time, and so I've been Joe ever since.

The more I remember, the more I can remember. The year we stopped switching names was the same year our parents got kidnapped on a cruise in the Pacific, became political prisoners, and never came back. Once they were gone, we were supposed to get adopted by the government, but my brother Marcus figured out a way around it. Marcus was only thirteen at the time, just five years older than Alvin and me, but he was the one who tracked down Uncle Ruby and convinced him to become our guardian. Uncle Ruby was officially supposed to be living with us in Los Angeles, but he had a girlfriend and a job in New York, so he wasn't around much at all—mostly just for a week in the summer. But he didn't mind lying to Social Services, and Marcus knew how to forge his signature, so we got along okay without him.

Alvin and I were mostly on our own. Marcus would sometimes try to tell us what to do, but it never worked out well, and so it was usually just the two of us. We spent every day together: maybe at the park, or at the beach, or trying out some new idea Alvin had. Alvin was a pretty big inventor, so we spent a lot of time working on his new concepts or building complicated pranks that he'd thought up. We were seventeen when Alvin met a girl on the Santa Monica beach, fell in love, and ran away with her to Tennessee.

After Alvin left, my life got so boring that I can barely remember anything I did. I guess I just woke up every morning, got hungry and thirsty, hung out at McDonald's, missed Alvin, played poker, missed Alvin, played ball. Every now and then I'd get the feeling that something else might eventually happen to me, but it never lasted very long, and I mostly wished time would pass faster until he came back. In December I turned eighteen without him—the first birthday that we didn't celebrate together.

I was supposed to be taking this GED course so I wouldn't have to start high school all over again. But the class seemed like it would be totally impossible to understand, and so I spent most of my time playing poker. I liked going to poker rooms because it was a chance to use my fake ID, and because poker is the main thing I remember about my father, how carefully he tried to teach it to me, even though I constantly forgot the rules.

This one time I saw an old man die at the poker table, right in the middle of the hand. He just leaned over and fell onto his cards, and when the dealer tried to wake him, we realized he was dead. While we waited for an ambulance, everyone crowded around to see what he had. It wasn't much, but he caught a really lucky straight on the last card and ended up winning the whole pot. When the dealer said the money would be sent on to the old man's family, this bald guy sitting next to me started getting really angry, because he'd had a pair of aces when the old man made his straight, and he thought you should have to be alive to win a pot. He wouldn't let it go, and eventually they had to call the floor man over. I only remember this so well because it was the same day Alvin finally called—the day things started happening to me again.

I knew it was Alvin as soon as my cell phone rang, because he'd bought that phone for me the day he left, and nobody else knew the number. I'd been carrying it around for months, hoping he would call, but now that it was finally ringing I couldn't seem to turn it on. I pushed all the buttons I could find, and it just kept ringing and ringing, and I started to get angry, and strangled the phone a little bit, until the bald guy next to me noticed what was happening. "Are you trying to answer your phone?"

"It's broken."

"It's not broken. You just don't know how to answer it."

He took my phone and messed with it for a while. The next thing I knew I was talking to Alvin.

"Hi Alvin."

"Joe," he said. "First let me apologize for never calling you for half a year. I've been employed all this time, so my schedule has been very demanding."

Right away I noticed that his voice was different. He sounded tired and sad and far away. I thought he might be calling from the bottom of a well.

"I miss you, Alvin."

"You are also someone I miss," he said. "What are you doing right now?"

"Playing cards."

"For money?"

4

"Yes."

"Good for you, Joe. I hoped you'd be doing the most irresponsible thing. Are you in shape for a trip?"

"What kind?"

"We'd go extremely far away. For a very long time."

"Would I have to work at all?"

"Hardly at all. And you won't have to talk to anybody you don't want to. It'll be like it was before I left. Tonight I'll tell you all about it."

"You're here?"

"I think I'm in New Mexico. I've been driving for fifteen hours straight. But I'll be there by tonight. Where are you sleeping these days?"

"In Marcus's apartment."

"Dammit." I could hear Alvin growling into the phone. "Tell me another place that you know how to get to."

I told him about the McDonald's near Marcus's apartment. He said that he would find it. "Eight o'clock," he said.

"I can't believe it finally happened. You came back."

"Of course I came back. Were you doubting me?"

"I talk to you sometimes, when you're not here," I said.

"You do?"

"It happens almost every week."

He coughed into the phone. Now I remember that he sounded terrified. I didn't think about it then. "Tonight I'm sure that you'll explain this bizarre piece of news," he said.

"Remember, just the two of us."

We said our good-byes and I turned off my phone. The bald man was tugging at my sleeve, and I realized that everyone at the table was staring at me. I took a second to remember where I was. This was the biggest card room in Los Angeles. There were probably a hundred poker tables in there, and a thousand players, and nobody ever left except to go outside and smoke, even when the fire alarms were going off.

"Come on, the action is to you," said the bald man.

I looked down at my cards. I'm sure they weren't very good, but now I was on this very happy and excited tilt. I bet, and raised, and re-raised, and then bet again. While someone else was scooping up the pot, the bald man pulled my sleeve again. "I shouldn't tell you this because I've won so much money from you," he said. "But you're the worst poker player that I've ever seen. What are you doing here? Why can't you lay down a hand?"

"I like it here."

"No. You're wasting all your time in here. Get out of here. Just get married and start having babies."

I knew this was excellent advice, even if I'd forget it instantly, but when I tried to thank him he just made a face like he'd eaten something terrible. "Old man dies during the hand and still hits a straight on the river," he said, disgusted. "Unbelievable. That should have been my pot. Come on, the action is to you."

He pulled my sleeve, and again the whole table was staring at me. I looked down at my horrible cards. Alvin always taught me that two seconds was the right amount of time to think about anything. "Any shorter and you're basically just living like an animal," he'd say. "Any longer and you're going to miss something else." I looked down at my horrible cards. *Just play with them*, I thought. *They're not so bad.*

When I finished losing all my money for that day, I rode the bus home to Marcus's house. Summer was starting, and so all this hot air was blowing through the bus. I always liked how the air in Los Angeles tasted, even though everyone said it was bad for you. Marcus rented an apartment right over the hill, in the valley. He was twenty-three years old and six foot eight, even taller than I was, and he was finishing college, where he went on a basketball scholarship. Marcus always accomplished everything he made a plan for, and he was full of important and practical advice.

Marcus always kept his apartment incredibly cold, to keep his metabolism operating more efficiently. The whole place was covered in thick carpet, and the vacuum cleaner lines were always fresh. You had to be careful in there because he had mousetraps all over the place. I found him in the kitchen, revving the blender and yelling at the business news on television. As soon as I walked in, he turned everything off and asked me, "Is Alvin coming into town?"

That was a pretty amazing thing for him to ask, because I knew Alvin would never have called him. But Marcus always seemed to know his whole life before it happened to him. Everything he did had been planned out for years. I put my book bag down. "Hi Marcus."

"Don't ignore me. Did he finally call you on that pathetic cell phone of yours?"

I was hoping that he'd forget about this subject and start talking about something else, but he just sat there waiting for me to answer while he poured himself a big yellow foamy glass from the blender. Marcus was always drinking something disgusting to make himself jump higher.

"Should I really tell you?"

"Tell me."

"Alvin called my cell phone. We talked for a while, and then we hung up."

"Did he say he was coming to town?"

"I think so."

"Are you going to see him?"

"We're having dinner in an hour."

"Just the two of you?"

"I think so."

"Is he planning to stop by?"

"I don't know."

"You don't know, or you don't think so?"

"I don't think he's planning to stop by."

"Did he ask how I was doing?"

"No, Marcus."

Marcus nodded slowly and took an angry drink of foam. I can remember this one time, when we were all a bunch of little kids, when he had tried to throw Alvin out a window, and another time when Alvin had tried to kill Marcus with some poison he'd made. They'd hated each other for so long that I couldn't even remember why.

"He probably knows I wouldn't see him anyway," said Marcus. "Not until he gives me about fifteen different apologies. For dumping you here, for example, just so he can chase some strange girl halfway across the country. Do you think I planned on housing my dropout younger brother while I took advantage of my college years? Do you think it was part of the plan that I made?"

"It probably wasn't."

I had no idea what plan Marcus had made, even though he told it to me all the time.

"Alvin is bad for you," he said. "Why can't you keep this in your head? You're like a dog who bangs his head into the same mirror every morning."

"I know, Marcus."

"Say it."

"Alvin is bad for me."

"Do I have to tattoo it on your chest, or can you keep that

in your head for one night?"

"Of course I can."

Marcus drank again until the outside of his mouth was totally covered in yellow foam. "Because he'll try to uproot you again. I'm guessing his life has just fallen apart. Do you want a cookie, Joe?"

I nodded. Marcus keeps my cookies in the freezer, because he knows I like them all frozen and crunchy. He locks the freezer door so I won't eat them all. He took one out and held it up in front of me.

"First promise you'll try to resist him."

I promised. While I ate the cookie, I'm pretty sure Marcus told me everything Alvin was going to say to me that night, and what he would ask me to do, and how exactly to say no to him, a lot of terrific information, but I was pretty focused on the cookie at the time. When I finished, I stood up and picked up my book bag.

"Aren't you wondering how I guessed he was coming here?" asked Marcus.

"Okay."

"A girl called for Alvin this morning, and when I screened the call, she left a message."

"What did it say?"

"Do you think I have time to spend all day listening to messages that aren't even for me? All I heard before I deleted the message was that she was looking for him."

"You deleted the message?"

"When you see him, please remind Alvin that I'm not his personal secretary and that any messages left here for him will be automatically deleted."

"Okay. I'll tell him."

"Oh, and one more thing. Make it clear that I didn't want to see him anyway. I wouldn't have seen him even if he wanted to. Make sure he understands that it was my decision just as much as his."

"Of course."

While I waited for eight o'clock, I took a shower and re-packed my book bag. Then I watched some TV. There was a pretty good movie on about some astronauts trying to save the moon. It looked so fun that I decided to become an astro-naut. I probably only remember this because it was the last TV I ever watched in that apartment.

While I was trying to leave the building without seeing him again, Marcus came running out with a basketball under his arm. He had all his gym clothes on, and his high-tops were all laced up. He threw the basketball at my stomach.

"Let's play one quick game before you go."

"Right now?"

"It's on the way. You have time. And the courts will be empty."

"Why now?"

"I think I might finally have an edge on you."

"But I don't have my shoes."

"Just play in those. You always play in those. Nothing too intense. Just a fun, friendly game."

I didn't believe him. Basketball with Marcus was never fun or friendly. He had a way of making sure that both players felt bad almost all the time.

"I'm sorry, Marcus." I gave him a friendly little bounce-pass. "I don't want to get all sweaty. We'll play another time."

Life is so full of impossible things that I can't understand. When I passed Marcus the basketball, he snarled and kicked it way over the fence into the swimming pool next door. I started to walk away. He ran after me and grabbed my collar.

"You're so pathetic," he said. "You're just like his little puppy dog."

"Good-bye, Marcus."

"I have an important summer league game tomorrow. If you're not here when I get back, I'm going to change the lock, and you can never live here again."

"Okay. Good luck in your game."

"I'm serious this time. I'm telling you now so there won't be any confusion later. I want you to understand how deeply I oppose Alvin's influence on you."

"Thank you. And I promise not to forget it."

"When are you going to start growing up, Joe?"

"Good-bye, Marcus."

I walked about ten blocks to the McDonald's. I like McDonald's because it's always the same incredible food, and they have pictures of their menu everywhere, and you can find out what everything costs just by watching TV. The one near our house was especially good, because they served breakfast all the way until eleven-thirty, and they hadn't replaced the steak bagels with that nasty breakfast burrito yet, and they didn't care if you hung out there all day and refilled your soda cup a hundred times.

It was getting so much hotter in the valley, and I was sweating by the time I arrived. McDonald's is actually one of my favorite smells; it always makes me feel safe and warm and happy. I said hello to Francisco's little brother, who hung out there all day too, reading this geometry book that he had. Then I said hello to Francisco, who was behind the counter salting some fries.

"Hi Joe."

"Francisco," I said. "Alvin's coming back into town. We're having dinner, just the two of us."

"Your twin brother," he said. "That's great. That's wonderful."

Francisco never talked that much. I think he'd only been in L.A. for a year or two, and so he didn't know that many words yet.

"We're going to eat dinner, just the two of us."

"Congratulations."

"Maybe I'll jump over the counter and check out the equipment."

This was one of my favorite things to do, even though I'd only done it a couple of times. Francisco checked around a little, wondering where the manager was, and took a peek behind him at the girl squirting mayonnaise on a hamburger bun.

"Not right now," he said. "I don't want to get fired with Carmen watching."

"You should kiss her. One day you should just kiss her right on the lips."

"No. I can't."

I could always make Francisco blush. He was so in love with Carmen that he could barely even look in her direction.

"Just talk to her," I said. "How will you ever know if you don't try?"

It surprised me when I said that, because it's not something I'd usually say. I must have been pretty excited if I was giving Francisco all this advice out of the blue.

Alvin showed up really late, and I'd already refilled my Coke three times by the time I saw him pull into the parking lot. I expected him to look exactly like he did the day he left Los Angeles, so happy and excited, with the pockets of his sweatshirt still filled with sand and his hair sticking up everywhere, as if falling in love had shocked him right in the heart. But now he looked just as different as he'd sounded on the phone—older and worried and tired. Even his car looked more beat up than I remembered it.

He had this big orange doggie with him now. I watched them from the window as Alvin walked all around the parking lot cleaning up after the dog with this plastic bag he had. He was really careful about it, very professional and thorough. But the dog just sat there watching him like it was bored, and it even stretched out on the ground at one point. I remember getting really angry and wanting to go over there and strangle the dog for not being more grateful for what Alvin was doing. And then suddenly I felt like jumping over the counter and running through the kitchen and out the back of the McDonald's and never coming back, and letting Alvin wait for me all night, just to show him how I'd felt when he stuck me here with Marcus to go off and be in love in Tennessee. When that feeling went away, I cleared my tray and threw away my Coke and went outside to meet him. "Alvin," I said. "Alvin, over here!"

I remember so well how he looked then, with the doggie lying next to him and the little baggie in his hand. He was all sunburned and peeling all over, like he'd been at the beach for a year. His green eyes had turned a little gray, and his hair was almost covering them. I don't think he'd had a haircut since the last time I'd seen him. I found out later that he'd been driving for two days without sleeping, and I'd never seen him look so tired. But he smiled when he saw me, and he looked at me so carefully, and I could feel him having such important thoughts about me, and finally he asked, "Joe, how is it that you never change?"

"Do we hug each other now?"

He nodded. I hugged him. He smelled like a cough.

"How's your book bag?" he asked.

"It's good."

"How did you do in the poker game today?"

"I have no idea."

"There you go," he said. "Boy, it's good to see you, Joe."

"Where did this dog come from?"

Alvin looked down at the dog, which was sprawled on the sidewalk, licking the slime running out of its nose. Alvin scratched the doggie underneath the chin. "He's teaching me loyalty. A man can only learn true loyalty from a dog."

"Where did you get him?"

"I found him down by the tracks, chasing trains. I knew he wouldn't live long doing that, so I decided to adopt him. I thought it might be fun to train him. But it's not the same as raising you."

"Is he fast?"

"Pretty fast. Mostly he just loafs around. I've been calling him Max."

"Are you hungry? Do we go inside and eat?"

"Not here," said Alvin. "But good for you, Joe. You still

don't know McDonald's is the worst possible place to eat food."

I always tune out in the passenger seat of a car. I go into a little trance, and when I get to where I'm going, I have no idea how. Actually I'm like this almost every second of my life. I don't know which way we drove that night. I can remember that we were on Ventura Boulevard as it was getting dark, and the street was all crowded with people and cars, and the air was blowing out of all these restaurants, carrying exciting smells into my nose, and I was starting to get hungry. On the way Alvin asked me about the imaginary conversations I'd been having with him. I told him it had only been a few times, when I especially missed him, and that maybe it happened because we were twins.

"What do we talk about?"

"We usually just joke around, remembering old times. Sometimes you try to get me to play pranks on Marcus, like put ice down his shirt while he's sleeping. Is this a bad sign? Does it mean I'm going crazy?"

"No, no. In fact, good for you, Joe. I'm always happy to be the subject of insane hallucinations. What else do I say?"

I tried to think. It hadn't happened for a while. "Sometimes you apologize to me."

"For what?"

"For leaving, I guess. Sometimes you give me little puzzles that I never solve. On my first day of class, you convinced me to skip it and play poker instead."

"What class? Since when do you take a class?"

"Marcus is making me study for the GED."

"Marcus. Of course." Alvin hated Marcus so much that it made him drive less carefully.

"If I don't pass, he says I have to start high school all over again."

"Or else?"

"He kicks me out into the street."

"There's Marcus in a nutshell," said Alvin. "He thinks they teach the secrets of the world in school. How often do you go?"

"The casino is right on the way," I said. "So far I haven't gone at all."

"God bless you, Joe. And now it makes no difference what Marcus thinks. You're not stuck with him anymore."

"Because you're not leaving again."

"Because we're both leaving. Now, what kind of building is this?"

Somewhere in there we'd left the car, and we were walking on a pretty quiet street. Most of the other stores were closing up. Alvin had the doggie on a leash in one hand, and in the other he carried this little green cloth suitcase. I took a look into the window.

"I see tables. Chairs. Waiters."

"And so?"

"It's a restaurant."

"Bingo. And next to the restaurant?"

"A motel." It was so fun to be with him again.

"Jackpot," said Alvin. "This is the White Palms Motel. Wanna say it?"

"The White Palms Motel."

"Take a good look. Burn it in. This is where I'm staying."

Alvin tied the doggie to a street lamp and we sat down at a table outside, in this little forest of metal heat lamps. The waitress brought us two big waters right away, which always impresses me, and I stared at the menu for a while, just for fun.

"Don't worry, they have cheeseburgers," said Alvin. "Now give me your opinion on this shirt."

I took a good look at this very stiff plastic shirt he had on. It didn't look comfortable at all, but I didn't want to hurt his feelings. "It reminds me of a Frisbee."

"One hundred percent biosynthetic materials. Completely indestructible. You can wash it with shampoo, right in the sink, and it will dry in seven minutes, guaranteed. I bought it on my way down here in a store for people who always think the world is going to explode and we will have to live like futuristic savages. I bought one for you too. You want to try it on?"

"Okay."

Alvin pulled another shirt out of his suitcase. This one was bright yellow, but otherwise exactly like his. "While I was paying for these shirts, the cashier gave me this real knowing look and told me, 'Wise purchase, brother,' and I was like, 'You know it, brother,' just so he wouldn't stick me with some galvanized steel dagger he'd hammered out in his basement."

The waitress came over and stood there until we finished talking. "Will you guys be ordering food?"

"We have to," said Alvin. "If we don't keep buying things, the whole economy will collapse. And it's the only way you'll let us sit here."

"Do you have cheeseburgers?" I asked.

"We certainly do."

"I'll have one of those, please."

"I forgot to read the menu," said Alvin. "But I'd just like to eat some chicken that's been cooked all the way through. You can surprise me with the details."

The waitress looked worried. She didn't hate Alvin yet, but I knew she might soon. She wrote on a pad for a while. "Any appetizers for you guys?"

"Do you have nachos?" Alvin wanted to know.

"Yes."

"With guacamole?" I asked.

The waitress nodded and wrote it down, and I remember that she smiled at me before she went away. I liked her. I thought about becoming a waiter while I buttoned up my new shirt. It fit me pretty well, except for the sleeves, but I already wanted to be out of it. It felt like I was wearing armor. "I think my arms are too long."

"Your arms have always been damn long. Do you still play basketball all day?"

"Some days."

"Still better than Marcus?"

I thought it over. Lately I hadn't seen Marcus play. "Probably."

"Good for you," said Alvin. "Good for you for squandering your gifts. Good for you for having insane dietary restrictions. Good for you for not being able to read. Good for you for carrying a cell phone no one ever calls. Good for you for hauling around the same book bag your whole life. Boy, I've missed you, Joe. Nobody changes less for the world than you do." He got up and stood on his chair. This is actually how I picture Alvin whenever I think about him, looking down on me with his arms spread, swaying back and forth like a ghost.

"Gifts are made to be squandered," he said. "We are meant to use them up and waste them, not to parlay them into a basketball scholarship. Never learn, never remember. Life is as short as a building on fire."

He looked a little sick, and lost his balance climbing down. "I'm going to tell you my idea now," he said. "The idea is that you and I will take these shirts and throw out all our other shirts, and then go sailing all around the world."

"On a boat?"

"On a boat, Joe. Everybody has a secret dream they never speak to anyone. This is mine. I never mentioned it before because it seemed impossible."

"We'd be sailors."

"I'd never make any plan that would require us to hold down steady jobs. No, if we sail, we sail like princes. Our own boat, with our own crew. If anything we'll be captains, but only when we feel like it. Eighteen is old enough to be a captain in most countries where we'll be going."

"You have a boat now?"

"I can buy one." Alvin slid his little suitcase across the table and unzipped it so I could see inside. I have no idea how much money was really in there, but it was obviously too much to ever count. "If we play our cards right, this money can be a boat by tomorrow morning."

I never asked Alvin where he got so much money, but I have a feeling that he might have told me the whole story right then and there, while I was sitting there staring at it. If I had just paid attention, then everything might have turned out differently. But I was so stunned by how much cash was in that bag that I missed everything he said. Then I smelled my cheeseburger; the waitress was coming back over. Alvin zipped up the bag and put it down next to his chair. He didn't talk again until she'd gone away.

"I've checked into some prices, Joe. We have enough to sail like princes for a year or two and then retire in comfort anywhere we choose. There are beaches in Brazil where the water is warmer than your bathtub."

"And never come back?"

"What do you have here that you can't leave behind?"

I didn't like being put on the spot, but I tried my best to come up with an answer. "I was thinking about becoming an astronaut."

"Then you're in the wrong place. There's no space program in Los Angeles. But most of the finest astronauts of all time started out as sailors. We can certainly put your training on our itinerary."

"Marcus is here."

"Marcus." Alvin started to get angry. "What did he tell you? That I'm bad for you?"

I nodded.

"That my life had probably fallen apart? That I'd try to talk you into something stupid? That you shouldn't go along with it?"

Now that I heard Alvin repeat it all, I could remember that Marcus had told me all of these things. "Yes."

"Did you believe him?"

"I can't remember."

"Joe?"

"I can't swim. Would we have to do a lot of swimming?"

"I need you, Joe."

I'd never heard him say that before, so I didn't know how much I'd enjoy hearing it. I'd never been on a sailboat before, and I didn't know anything about the ocean. I didn't know if we'd be fishing for whales, or living in some house made out of snow, or if we'd end up floating down a river through the jungle somewhere, but it was exciting to think about sailing around the whole world with him. And I believe we really would have done it too, if we'd had a little more time.

"I need you," repeated Alvin. "Right now you're just about the only person I can stand. I've had some pretty bad luck lately."

"What happened?"

"She's gone." He put his hands over his eyes and his whole body started to shake. For a second I thought he was laughing, but then I realized he was sobbing all over the place. He tried to cover his eyes, but the tears came out from under his palms. I started crying too.

"Stop it," he said. "Don't cry, Joe."

"I can't help it." I wiped my face and blew my nose into a napkin, but I still couldn't stop. This always happened to me whenever Alvin cried, and there was nothing I could do. "I'm sorry," I said.

"Please stop. I can't take it."

"Then you stop. You stop crying."

"You don't even know what you're crying about."

"It's not my fault," I said. "You shouldn't have started crying in the first place."

"Okay, I'm stopping. I'm stopping now. Goddammit, Joe."

Alvin took a few deep breaths and managed to calm himself down. Pretty soon I stopped too. "Okay, no more crying from anybody. Have you ever seen me smoke a cigarette?"

"No."

"Well, you're about to. I just started today." Soon Alvin had a cigarette in his mouth. He took a pack of matches off the table. "They say a cigarette takes fifteen minutes off your life, but a sitcom takes twice that long, and it's still a half hour well spent. What am I doing?" he said. "I have a perfectly good lighter, so why am I trying to strike a match? And why on my lighter? Why strike a match on a perfectly good lighter?"

He stood up. I knew he wanted to climb on the chair again, but he realized it was a bad idea, so he just stood over the table, rocking back and forth, and looking down at me. "A grown man should never strike a match on a lighter. There is no place for it in a functioning person's life. It means that something has gone terribly wrong." He sort of fell back into his chair, and used the lighter on the cigarette, and tried a puff on it, and made a miserable face, and coughed up all this smoke into my eyes. "Julia's gone."

"Who?"

"The girl, Joe. The girl I ran away with. She left me. I wasn't strong enough to keep her, in the end." He held his empty glass up to one eye, and then the other one, until he wasn't crying anymore. His eyes were all puffy and red. He tried to smile. "But there is certainly a bright side. Suppose we decided to get married some day. I get a normal job. We take out a loan to buy a nicer car. In middle age she starts to cook these watery soups. We raise a child with a predictable sense of humor. I'm probably lucky the whole situation went so horribly wrong."

"But what happened?"

Alvin took a long, careful look around the room. Then he leaned across the table and whispered, "I went a little bit on tilt."

The restaurant. The cheeseburger. The waitress with the funny, worried eyes. Outside afterward the street was dark and quiet. Alvin squinted up and down the sidewalk as he untied the doggie. "Do me a favor, Joe. Go around the corner and see if anybody's been waiting for us in the parking lot."

"Why?"

"It'll be fun. Just pretend you're a spy."

I walked around the corner. The parking lot was even

darker than the street, but a little farther down, behind the restaurant, I remember that the ground was sparkling. When I got a little closer, I saw it was because of all these bottle caps in the street. They'd been run over so many times they'd been pushed into the asphalt, and now they were part of the street. I guess it was the moon that made them glitter like that. Those bottle caps were pretty, and so I went over to look at them.

When I got back, Alvin was lying on the hood of the car, sleeping. The doggie was licking his arms. When I shook him, he sat up right away and said, "Have you driven at all lately?"

"I could try."

"Okay, okay. I'll drive."

It was extremely dangerous, the way he drove me home. It seemed almost like he was hoping we would get into an accident, and at the same time he was trying to tell me this complicated puzzle about three doors and a lion. I couldn't make head or tail of it. Somehow we made it to Marcus's apartment without crashing into anything. Alvin parked the car but didn't turn it off.

"Is Marcus here?"

"He went to bed early, I think. He has a big game tomorrow."

"Oh yeah? Where at?"

"I don't remember."

"Marcus go away a lot?"

"Pretty often."

"He seems okay?"

"I think he seems okay."

"I bet he's full of practical advice. I bet he presents you with a pamphlet on achieving excellence. I wish I could stand to be in the same room with him. Here's the thing about Marcus . . ." Alvin rested his head on the steering wheel. He looked so tired. I think he'd forgotten what he wanted to say. Then he sat up suddenly and looked at me. "I've done something pretty stupid," he said. "That's why it's a very good time to sail around the world where nobody can find me. But I can't imagine going without you. I need you, Joe."

"Could you say that one more time?"

"Please tell me that you're coming."

I felt like I should wait before I answered him. I knew I was breaking all my promises to Marcus, but I couldn't remember what any of them were. I couldn't remember anything I'd been doing since Alvin left, except for that I'd been sort of waiting for my life to start again. Tomorrow the sun would come up and we'd be a team again. I put my hand on his shoulder. "Of course I'll come," I said. "When have I not come?"

Alvin hugged me. "Good for you, Joe." I couldn't hug him back well because my seat belt was still on, but I could feel that he was shivering. "I'm sorry I left you with him for so long."

"That's okay."

We finished hugging. I unsnapped my seat belt and opened the door.

"Do you understand why I had to do it?" he asked.

"You fell in love."

"That's right. I fell in love with Julia. And so I really had no choice."

Later on I found out exactly what Alvin meant, because I fell in love with Julia too, but at the time I couldn't understand it. I got out of the car. "Thanks for driving me home."

"Just remember to charge up your cell phone tonight. I'll call you when it's time to leave for the airport. We'll have to find some plane tickets somewhere. Don't forget to pack your new shirt."

"I'll put it in my book bag."

"I'll see you tomorrow. Sleep tight, Joe."

"Goodnight, Alvin."

After he drove away, I walked back to the McDonald's one more time to say good-bye. They were just barely still open, and Francisco was the only cashier left. I jumped over the counter without even asking and pumped his hand while I gave him the good news, and said my good-byes. Then I told him, "Just kiss her!" and ran home to pack a little bit, my wallet and some socks and underwear, and a couple of extra shirts. I hoped that Alvin would understand that I didn't want to wear that plastic yellow shirt for the rest of my life. I plugged in my cell phone so it would charge like crazy all night long, and as I was falling asleep with the phone in my hand, I started to remember the whole day. I'd ridden the bus in the rain. The angry bald man fixed my phone. Marcus kicked the basketball over the fence. Francisco. Carmen. Alvin brought that doggie in a car. The restaurant. There were heat lamps. Alvin cried and tried to smoke a cigarette. The bottle caps that sparkled in the street. Life is so full of impossible things that I can't understand. Now I remember that when I went to check the parking lot, there *had* been someone waiting there in a parked car, sitting quietly and watching. But I got distracted by those bottle caps and forgot to take a second look, or say anything to Alvin when I got back. Why couldn't I remember that before?

CHAPTER TWO

That night I dreamed we had sailed all the way to Japan, and Alvin was standing in a kimono with his arms spread on top of a windy mountain, while I chopped up a pile of wood. I woke up under Marcus's orange quilt, staring at my wall, and I could smell the swimming pool outside the apartment building. While I lay there for a minute remembering where I was, I suddenly got very nervous and confused, like I wasn't quite sure that my life would work out. It only lasted for a minute or two. When it was over I got up and got dressed, packed my book bag, and then sat on the bed waiting for Alvin's call.

He never called. I waited the whole morning and some of the afternoon, and then decided to go to his motel, but

I couldn't remember its name or anything about where it was, so I spent that whole terrible day walking lost around the valley, sweating, looking everywhere for that motel, and I never found it. By the time it started to get dark, I was dizzy and my feet were tired. My head hurt, and when I saw a fountain in the middle of this little park, I realized how thirsty I was. It was the kind of fountain that shoots up water when you don't expect it, and it had this pretty decent pool around it. The whole place smelled a little bit like trash because of a dumpster too close by. Next to the dumpster two kids were smashing bottles in a language that I couldn't understand. Behind them I saw a couple throwing bread at a huge crowd of pigeons, who were fighting over it like little children. Someone had thrown out this terrible sofa right in the middle of the park, and a dog came limping by, dragging one leg, and everything out there was dirty or breaking or broken, and I was lost and I had no idea what to do. I dunked my head into the fountain and yelled into the water for a while, and then I just started gulping like crazy, drinking as much of the fountain as I could, and the more I drank the thirstier I got. I stayed down there gulping and yelling and swallowing water until I knew I was about to drown. When I finally came up for air, Alvin was standing there laughing at me.

"God bless you, Joe."

"Why are you laughing?"

"Because I knew you'd forget the name of the motel."

"Remind me one time."

"The White Palms."

"That's it. That's the only part I couldn't remember." I was still panting like a dog. "Am I close?"

"We're seven miles away. God bless you, Joe."

"I looked all day for you. What happened? Why didn't you call?"

"I changed my mind. The trip is off."

"What?"

"That's what I came here to tell you. I decided to go by myself."

"Why?"

"I can't make you live my dream, can I?"

"But I wanted to go."

"No, you'd hate the ocean, believe me. You can't even swim, for one thing, and you wouldn't like all that traveling. The farther we went, the nastier things you'd have to eat. And you've built up a nice life for yourself here."

"Dammit," I said.

"Hey," said Alvin. "Don't get angry."

"I can't help it."

"Find a way."

"I just really wanted to go. Why can't I go?"

"Because the decision has already been made."

"You couldn't change your mind again?"

Alvin shook his head. "Impossible. I'm already gone."

"What?"

"I'm already gone, Joe. I'm on a flight to Miami. I found the perfect sailboat, and we're crewing up this afternoon. I'll be on the ocean by sundown!"

I couldn't make any sense of what Alvin was saying, and then suddenly I understood. I wasn't talking to the real Alvin. I took his hands and, sure enough, they felt cold. It was like taking the hands of a statue. This is why I tried not to touch Alvin when he appeared like this. He always felt cold in a way that could never be warmed up.

"Isn't that strange?" he said. "I don't feel cold at all."

"Why did you have to leave so early?"

"I found a last-minute deal on a flight that was too good to pass up. But I'll be back in town before you know it. We'll have an incredible time."

Something about this situation felt familiar, and then I remembered that Marcus had also predicted this, that after Alvin convinced me to give up my whole life for him, everything would fall apart, and he would abandon me again.

"You lied to me," I said.

"Lied to you? Now you've stumped me. You'll have to explain."

"You said you needed me."

"That's so wonderful, Joe. God bless you for saying that out loud. You don't remember the general direction of the food you ate last night, but you claim total recall of every single word I spoke to you. Besides, what's the difference? I'm still here, aren't I?"

"It's not the same."

"Come on, don't have your first bad mood right now. Do you remember the name of the motel?"

"Remind me one more time."

"The White Palms Motel."

"The White Palms Motel."

"It's truly amazing how far away you are. We're not even in the same zip code."

"Why am I going to the motel if you're not even there?"

"Max is still there."

"Who?"

"My dog," said Alvin. "If I try to take him sailing around the world, it's very likely that he'll drown, so you'll have to take over until I get back. He's waiting for you in my room."

"What do I do with him?"

"Food, water, and a walk or two, and otherwise he runs completely on his own. Dogs need even less to stay alive than we do. I'd call it a favor if it weren't so easy. If you want my car, the keys are always in the muffler. Are you ready to look for a taxi, or are you going to drink the rest of that water?"

"Just a little more."

I bent down for one last long drink of water. When I

came up for air, Alvin had disappeared. The two boys had finished smashing all their bottles, and now they were trying to throw each other into the fountain. Everybody else was gone.

"The White Palms Motel." I repeated the name out loud until I found a cab driver to say it to. It wasn't a cheap cab ride. I really had walked a long way. I recognized the motel as soon as I arrived, and the little restaurant next door where we had eaten the night before. Alvin's car was in the parking lot. I guess it was my car now. I'd never been inside a motel before, though I'd seen them plenty of times on TV. The lobby was a little like an old movie theater, with the counter and everything, except it was a less friendly place and smelled more like cigarettes. The framed pictures on the walls were all photographs of the motel over the years. Part of the ceiling was covered with a white sheet that flapped in the breeze from outside. Behind the front desk, the manager was watching TV with the sound off while he played some classical music on this tiny radio. He was already angry with me. I guess Alvin hadn't told anyone he was leaving the dog behind in his room, and the dog had been barking all day, and nobody wanted to go in there to calm him down.

"Pretty scary surprise for the maid," he said. "You're not supposed to have dogs in this place anyway. Another hour and I would've called the pound."

I was used to people being furious at me for something

Alvin had done. He made a lot of people angry. That was just the way he lived. I lived my whole life on tilt also, even worse most of the time, but it was different with Alvin because it seemed like he did it on purpose. "Don't worry, I'm here to take the dog away."

"Who are you, his friend?"

"His twin brother."

"You don't look it."

"Well, I am."

"Can you prove it?"

I did the best I could. I could never get a driver's license in a million years, but I had my ATM card, and it satisfied him once he'd squinted at it for a while.

"I'll go and get the key. Will you calm that girl down?"

"What girl?"

"I figured you would know her. She got here an hour ago, looking for him. She's totally hysterical. Three times already I've had to stop her from calling Missing Persons."

"He's not missing. He flew to Florida to buy a boat."

"Well, you'd better explain that to her. Who's going to pay for the day the dog spent in the room?"

"I guess I am. That card should probably work." I'd given him my bank card, but I mostly used it at the ATM, so I was trying like hell to remember my signature.

"I'll go and get the key. She's in the Hawaiian Lounge, in the back. Please try to calm her down. The last thing we need is a bunch of police running around here. It's just not how I want to spend my birthday."

That's when I noticed he had a little plate behind the counter with a cupcake on it, with a little candle that still hadn't been lit. After he disappeared into the back, I went into the Hawaiian Lounge. It was mostly just a television and an empty watercooler, but they did have a palm tree growing in the middle, planted in an enormous coconut. This girl was sitting on the rim of the coconut, holding a magazine she wasn't reading. I noticed her hair right away, because it was such a bright, strong red color that I'd never seen before. Her legs were so long that at first I thought she might be as old as Marcus. But the closer I got, the younger she looked, until finally we were face-to-face and I saw that she was about my age. Her eyebrows and lashes were lighter than her hair, almost blonde, and she had obviously been crying pretty recently, so her eyes were big and wet and green and a little bit wild. She had such an emotional face. I don't know. I just always thought Julia was really beautiful.

"Are you okay?"

"Who are you?"

"I'm Alvin's brother Joe."

"Really?" She blew her nose into some tissues and dried off her face with her sleeve. I waited while she took a better look at me. "But you don't look like him at all."

"I know."

"Your whole face is different. How come Alvin never mentioned that?" She wouldn't stop looking at my face, and then she reached out her fingertips, and for a second I was sure she was about to touch my cheek, but she stopped herself halfway, and then somehow we wound up shaking hands. "I'm Julia."

"From Tennessee."

"That's right."

I didn't mention it, but she also looked completely different than I'd pictured her. I'd always imagined Julia as a dragon who had been eating Alvin for six months and then finally spit him out. I'd never really thought of her as a real person. But now I could see why Alvin had fallen in love with her on the beach that day. It was exciting just to have her looking at me.

"I'm supposed to calm you down."

"For who, the manager? I can't get that guy to take me seriously. What did he say about me?"

"He just asked me to talk to you."

"I'll calm down when Alvin comes back."

"He's not coming back."

"He's not?"

"He's probably in the middle of the ocean by now. He left this morning to go sailing all around the world. "

"How do you know?"

"He told me."

39

"Really?" Julia chewed her hair a little as she thought this over. "So he finally went. I can't believe it. I never thought he would actually go." She gave me this goofy grin and shot herself in the head with an imaginary pistol. "Now I feel like an idiot."

"Why?"

"I got totally hysterical, flying out here like a maniac for no reason. Ruining that poor man's birthday. My parents think I'm at a roller-skating festival with Angie. I don't even know if there is such a thing."

This was already the longest I'd ever talked to a girl I didn't already know, and I could easily have kept going too, but the manager came back with the key. He hadn't cheered up at all. We had to walk through the whole parking lot to the end of the motel, and then up this nasty yellow staircase to Alvin's room. We could hear the dog barking while the manager got the door open, but when we finally got into the room, it was totally empty and clean. This made everyone pretty confused, until we realized the dog had been locked in the bathroom all day. He recognized Julia as soon as she let him out, and tried to lick her hands while she tried to scratch his chin.

"Max," she said. "Did the maid lock you in there? Sit, Max!"

Max didn't sit right away, and so Julia had to sort of push his butt down. "I knew Alvin wasn't ready for a dog," she told him. "Who's supposed to take care of you now?"

"I am," I said.

"What?"

"Just until Alvin gets back."

"That's pretty nice of you."

"It is?"

"You're taking care of a dog he never should have adopt-ed in the first place, so he can go sailing around the world. Yeah, I'd say that's pretty nice."

It hadn't occurred to me, but now that Julia felt so strongly about it, it did seem like a pretty nice thing to do. I went over to pet the dog a little bit. His nose felt like an ice cube. He'd done this little poop on the floor of the bath-room, right next to the toilet and everything, and it didn't even smell too bad. I really think he handled himself pretty damn well, considering his situation. He was a pretty good dog so far. "So I'll just put the room on your card," said the manager.

"Okay."

"Hi," said Julia. "Are you really charging us for this room?"

"Have to," said the manager. "The dog's been here all day."

"But he's been locked in the bathroom. It's not like housekeeping needs to clean the whole place again."

"Excuse me for asking, but how old are you?"

"I worked in hotels since before I can remember," said Julia. "So I do know a couple of things. You're not supposed to ask your customers their age, for one thing. And you're not supposed to rip them off just because they're young, or because they cry a little in the lobby. The dog was in the bathroom the whole day. I know you won't even change the hand towels in here. And the place isn't even half full."

"I'm not going to stand here and argue with some hotel prodigy," said the manager. "I'll charge him for a quarter day. That's more than fair."

"That's so great," said Julia. "I think that was a really nice compromise." She gave him a big smile and took the doggie by the collar. "Seem fair to you, Joe?"

"Seems fair to me."

By the time we got back into the office, I'd remembered my signature pretty well. I hadn't practiced it at all since Alvin left, and so I thought I'd be more rusty, but it really did look quite beautiful and special there on the tiny white hotel bill.

"So now what?" said Julia. "I'm stuck here for two days. I've never traveled alone before, and I don't think I'm too good at it. I haven't eaten anything all day but peanuts."

"I drank an awful lot of water, but that's it."

"There must be a fun place to have dinner somewhere around here."

"I have a car," I said.

I never should have said "I have a car" so quickly like that, and with all that confidence, because I'd driven maybe three hours total in my life, and most of it was this one terrible day when Alvin stole Marcus's car, and I wound up destroying it, along with a couple of street signs. But I wanted to make sure I went wherever Julia was going.

Outside, it had become nighttime. While I stood there looking at Alvin's car, trying to remember how to drive, the doggie started licking my hand. I thought he might be hungry after a whole day locked in the hotel, so I got some money from an ATM and bought him some dog food from this little market on the corner, and he ate three cans, and threw up, and ate two more cans, and drank a little puddle of water, and peed with his leg in the air.

"I think he keeps his keys in the muffler," said Julia.

"That sounds familiar."

I couldn't think of any more excuses. I got the keys out of the muffler, threw Julia's bag in the backseat, and then we both got into the car. As soon as the door was open, Max jumped in and climbed into the back. The whole car smelled like a lawn, and the backseat was covered in doggie bones. Even before I got my door closed, Julia was already fixing her lipgloss in the mirror. She had no idea how nervous I was. I put the key into the ignition and turned it.

Life is so full of impossible things that I can't understand. I'll never be able to explain what happened next. I don't know if it was because the car reminded me so much of Alvin, or because Julia was there trusting that I knew what I was doing, but for whatever reason driving that car suddenly became something I could do. I was nervous for a block or so, trying to remember how I'd crashed before, so I could try to avoid it this time, when I suddenly got the hang of the whole thing. The wheel, the pedals, even the blinkers, it all made perfect sense to me, all at the same time. I can't remember anything about the day I learned to walk, but it must have been a very similar feeling. After a mile or so I even started to enjoy it, and I especially liked driving with Julia next me, chatting away like this was the most normal thing in the world.

"I like Los Angeles," she said. "I think Cecily would like it too."

Later I found out that Cecily was her sister, but I had no idea at the time. This is something I eventually got used to with Julia. She always talked to you as if you'd known her all your life. Suddenly she grabbed my arm.

"I think I just saw a really fun diner, right across the park. See? There's a man outside dressed up like a hot dog. I think I could really go for a nice tuna melt right now. Are you as hungry as I am, Joe? Did you know it's the first day of summer?"

The diner was full of little children with their parents. All the waiters and waitresses were dressed up like park rangers for some reason. We couldn't find any empty booths, so we sat on stools at this little round table that was barely big enough for our plates. Underneath the table, I remember that our knees were touching the whole time. We were waiting for my cheeseburger and Julia's tuna melt when she started talking about Alvin again. "I'm so happy he finally followed through on his sailing idea," she said. "I think maybe a nice long trip is exactly what he needs. He's been talking about it for so long. But Joe?"

"Yes?"

"Are you positive that's where he went?"

"He got on a plane this morning."

"That's so great," she said. "I'm just really proud of him for going. Though I do feel a little stupid now."

"Why?"

"No, I won't tell you. It's going to sound so arrogant."

"Okay."

"No, I'll tell you. I might as well just tell you. This is so embarrassing." When she got nervous Julia always talked a little faster. She kept taking ice out of her water and chewing it while she talked. "I thought Alvin might be suicidal," she said. "Isn't that ridiculous? When he called from the hotel last night, he kept saying good-bye, like it was the last time we would ever talk. He sounded so strange that I stayed up all night worrying, and he wouldn't answer his phone anymore, and so in the morning I got on the first plane I could find. Joe, are you positive Alvin went to Miami?"

"That's what he told me."

"That's so great, to follow through on a dream like that," said Julia. "I must be pretty stuck-up to think a boy would ever be suicidal over me."

"You mean because you left him?"

"Who said I left him?"

"That's what Alvin said."

"Did he really tell you that? Wow. Amazing how he thinks. I didn't break up with Alvin. He broke up with me. And all because I wouldn't blow off college and abandon my whole family to go sailing around the world with him." Julia's face had turned a little red. She had finished all the ice cubes in her water, and started in on mine. "When he first told me the idea, I thought he was joking. But he wouldn't let it go. Finally last week he tells me that it's now or never. I thought that was really unfair. He acted like I was making him leave. But the ultimatum was his idea, not mine. He's the one who drove off in the middle of the night. I have no idea why he'd tell you it was my decision."

When the waitress finally came back with our food, I realized how hungry I was. I dug into my cheeseburger right away. After a few bites I realized that Julia was just sitting there watching me.

"He never mentioned what a good listener you are," she said. "I feel like I've been jabbering on and on."

"What did he mention?"

"He said you were his favorite person. And he said you never changed."

"What else?"

"He never talked a lot about his family, to be honest. I know he didn't get along with Marcus, but he wouldn't talk about it. So you tell me something."

"Like what?"

"I don't know. Tell me a secret about you. Something most people wouldn't know."

I thought it over for a little while. "I don't know if it's a secret. But it's definitely something I don't usually mention."

"Go ahead. This sounds juicy."

"I can't eat anything except for pizza and cheeseburgers."

"That's it?"

"Plus a couple of desserts. Candy, cookies, things like that."

"But why?"

"I tried it for a little while when I was a kid. It was basically just a game at first, but then somehow I got stuck with it. My brother Marcus tried to have me hypnotized to make it go away, but it didn't work. Why are you laughing?"

It was the first time I'd made her laugh. I really didn't

care why she was laughing. It was the most attention she had paid to anything I'd said so far.

"It's just the strangest thing I've ever heard," she said. "What happens if you eat something else?"

"It tastes okay, I guess. It's basically like eating clay. If it's too spicy, sometimes I throw up. I can eat some other things sometimes, like pasta, if it tastes enough like pizza or a cheeseburger."

"It has to have cheese? You can't eat a regular hamburger?"

"If I get desperate. But it's not the same."

"That's such an unusual diet. I've never heard anything like that."

Julia put a little bit of tuna fish on her fork and held it out to me. "Why don't you taste this?"

"I won't like it."

"Try it once."

"Why?"

"Just try it for me, Joe."

I opened my mouth. After she fed me with the fork, Julia put her palm under my chin and gently pushed my mouth closed. This was the first time she'd touched my face. I felt like there was a fire underneath the table, where our knees were touching. Since I'd met Julia everything was so exciting I could barely stand it. I was so distracted that the tuna fish didn't even taste so bad, and for a second I thought I might actually swallow it, but in the end I couldn't quite do it. I spit the tuna fish out onto my plate.

"Almost," I said.

"It was a good try anyway."

"I almost did it," I said. "That was the closest I've come in a while."

"We'll try again sometime. Did you know licorice could be a straw? Here, look." Julia got out some licorice from her purse and showed me. For the rest of our dinner, we drank through licorice sticks, and it made her smile every single time. She never seemed to get tired of doing it, and so neither did I, and I would have been pretty happy to stay inside that diner all night long, but Julia remembered that we'd left the doggie in the car, so we paid the check and went outside.

"I need to find a place to stay," she said.

"Me too," I said.

"I thought you lived here."

"I lived with Marcus, but he told me if I wasn't home tonight I was officially kicked out. He might change his mind, but not if I wake him up."

This might have been a lie, for all I knew. Even if I did wake Marcus up, he'd probably just yell at me a little bit, and make up a few extra rules, and then everything would go back to the way it was before. But I wanted to stay with Julia, and so I didn't really care if anything I said was true.

"I don't think they'll take us back at the White Palms

Motel," said Julia.

"We'll find another room. It'll be easy." Now I was just saying anything that I could think of. "There are probably a million motels in Los Angeles."

"Is that too strange?" asked Julia. "Have you ever shared a room with someone you just met?"

"I've never even stayed in a motel before."

"It's cheaper than getting two rooms. So it's more responsible, in a way. Am I ridiculous, Joe? Would you tell me if you thought I was?"

"Why would you ask me that?"

"I've felt crazy all day. Like I have no idea what I'm going to do next. Could it be jet lag?"

"What?"

"It's not like I'd normally want to share a room with some boy I just met. But I feel like I've known you for more than two hours. And I'm scared to stay alone."

"We'll split it," I said.

"We'll split it right down the middle. I think that's a really good idea."

The first motel we tried wouldn't take dogs, but at the second place Julia managed to convince the night manager, by talking to her as a fellow hotel employee. While the manager was thinking about it, the doggie started licking her hand, and I think that's what eventually won her over. That's probably my favorite memory of Max, and it's usually what I picture when I think about him.

This motel room was smaller than the other one I'd seen. There was just enough room for one regular bed, and one sofa bed, and a TV. I remember that the freezing cold air pouring out of the vents in the walls smelled like it came out of somebody's basement. I filled up the ice bucket with water and gave it to the doggie, along with another can of food. I was so nervous that I couldn't think of anything to say, but luckily for me there was a television, so we lay on the bed for an hour and watched a movie about some people trying to get down from a mountain that's crawling with ghosts. Julia got really into the movie, and once or twice it stressed her out so much that she jumped up and turned off the TV. But she couldn't stand not watching either, so she'd always turn it right back on. When the movie was over, we unfolded the couch into this very lumpy bed, and I lay down to see how it felt. The mattress was really thin, and I could feel sharp pieces of metal underneath it, digging right into my back. I think I probably would have slept better on the couch, without unfolding it, but I didn't really care. I still couldn't believe that I'd be staying in this room all night with Julia, and nothing else made too much difference to me.

While I was trying out the mattress, Julia took her suitcase into the bathroom to get dressed for bed. She came out a few minutes later in this huge blue T-shirt and these incredible white shorts, and then just stood there for a while in the doorway watching me try to get comfortable. I think I was under the covers by then, but I was still wearing all my clothes because I was too nervous to even take my socks off.

"Can we leave the bathroom light on?" she said. "I can't sleep when it's completely dark."

"Go ahead."

Julia stayed there in the doorway for a second longer.

"I watched you eat today," she said. "You loved it. It made me so happy to watch you enjoy that cheeseburger so much." She patted the dog one more time and said, "Goodnight, Max," and climbed into her bed and pulled the blankets up under her chin. But I guess she really wasn't ready to sleep yet, because she didn't even close her eyes. After about a minute she asked me, "Did you ever play poker with Alvin?"

"It's the only card game that I know."

"He taught me how to play."

"Me too."

She turned on the light, and I went over to sit on the edge of her bed. We played poker for about an hour, using these M&Ms Julia had as chips. She won every game, and I could tell she'd learned to play from Alvin, because it felt the same as losing to him. I'd always liked playing with Alvin, because even though he always won, it always felt like we were both winning together, and that's how it was with Julia too.

After she won all the M&Ms, we split them up and ate them all. Then I went back to my horrible foldout sofa bed and she turned off the light, but I guess she still wasn't tired.

"I remember standing in the parking lot of the hotel, watching Alvin drive away," she said in the dark. "And I had a feeling I'd never see him again."

"He'll come back eventually. That's what happened the last time he left."

"When it comes to old boyfriends, they say it can go one of two ways. You either stay close to them forever or you never talk to them again."

I can still remember how quiet it was in that room. The air conditioner had shut off, and there weren't any airplanes overhead, or people jabbering outside, or anything. Julia's voice was quiet, almost a whisper, but it filled up the whole room.

"When Alvin left Tennessee, it was like I split off into two different lives," she said. "In one of those lives, I went with him, and I'm sailing around the tip of Florida right now. In the other life, I didn't go with him, but will always wonder if I should have, and that's the life I'm living in right now. I thought about it, Joe. I really did. But an eighteen-year-old girl can't just drop everything and run away."

"I would have gone with him," I said. "If he had let me."

"Last year I spent half a semester in Sweden," said Julia. "For the first month it was the most exciting place I'd ever been. And the second month I felt like I'd been there all my life. And the third month I got so homesick that I had to come home early. I'm not saying that being with Alvin was exactly like that. But he can be a lot to handle sometimes. I'm sorry that I keep going on about him."

"It's okay."

"Then I'll just go on a little longer. The first time I ever saw him he was reading a book on the beach. He was so focused on his book that he had no idea I was watching him. Then he reacted to something he was reading and spit into his book. Not even in an angry way. But something in the book made him want to spit, and he forgot where he was. Do you think that's why I went over to talk to him?"

"Sounds like something he would do."

"I think Alvin lived in a dream world most of his life. But anyway, I'm finished rambling about him now, I promise. Goodnight, Joe."

"Goodnight, Julia."

I never found a way to lie on that mattress that didn't hurt a lot, but I don't think that was the reason it took me forever to go to sleep that night. It felt as if more had happened to me that day than in my whole life up to that time, and so instead of sleeping I just lay there trying to remember it all. Sneaking out that morning. The terrible walk through the valley. Trying to drink the fountain, and then seeing Alvin there. The cab. The motel. The little birthday cupcake that the hotel manager had. Then Julia. I knew something about the way she talked about my brother felt familiar, and lying in the dark I finally realized that it reminded me of school, before I stopped going, how they always made us read books and discuss them. I never tried to read any of the books, but I listened to everyone else talk about them. The teacher was always bugging the kids to say important things about the books, and everyone except me eventually learned to do it. And that's how Julia talked about Alvin. I had never thought so hard about a person in my life, and I felt a little guilty for listening to her do it, and for thinking a little harder about him myself. I think maybe if Julia really loved Alvin, she wouldn't think about him quite so hard. And trying to understand him clearly wasn't helping her, because she was frowning as she slept, wrinkling up the whole top of her nose. I thought maybe if I went over and kissed the center of her forehead, it would smooth out her whole face, like shaking out a towel. But while I was deciding whether to actually do it, I finally fell asleep.

In the middle of the night, I woke up to find Julia talking again. She was lying on her back, moving her arms and legs like she was climbing a ladder. "What are we going to do?" she was saying. "I just have no idea how to handle this."

"What's wrong?"

She sat straight up in the bed, totally still. "Who's going

to make breakfast tomorrow? That's what I want to know. What are we going to eat?" She started to panic again, swinging her arms faster now. I got out of bed and went over to try to calm her down.

"We can go to McDonald's," I said. "Or we can go back to the same diner. We can go anywhere you want."

"It's going to be too late. We should have planned it earlier." Her eyes were wide open, but she wasn't looking at anything, just staring through the wall in front of her as if it wasn't there. I realized that Julia was still asleep. I'd seen Marcus do this a few times, but when he talked in his sleep, he never said more than a couple of words, and you could never understand him. Julia was different. She talked a lot, and you could understand her perfectly, and she'd tell you things she'd never say when she was awake.

"I promise we'll have enough breakfast," I said. "Everybody's going to get enough to eat."

"I don't understand how you two can be brothers."

"Who, me and Alvin?"

"How can you be his twin, when you're so much stronger than he is?"

"I don't know. I've always been really strong."

She wouldn't stop flailing around. None of her covers were tucked in anymore. "What exactly is our plan for food tomorrow morning? That's what nobody will tell me."

"I'm telling you right now."

"It's not like I want all this responsibility. But if I don't worry about it, who will?"

"I'm taking care of it. You're sleeping, Julia. Just try to close your eyes again."

She couldn't hear any of the words I said, but the sound of my voice seemed to be calming her down. "I'm going to take care of it," I said again, and then kept talking in this very gentle way, until gradually she stopped moving around so much. Eventually she lay completely still and closed her eyes. I tucked in her covers again, and then kissed her forehead just like I had wanted to all day, and she slept without talking for the rest of the night.

CHAPTER THREE

When I woke up it was already the afternoon and Julia was coming out of the bathroom wrapped in this big fluffy towel. Her hair was all wet and she smelled like shampoo. "Get up, Joe. We slept almost twelve hours."

"What's happening?"

"Shouldn't we go see if your brother will let you back in?"

That was the last thing I felt like doing, but I couldn't think of a way out. I got dressed, and gave some food to Alvin's doggie, and then we took the elevator down and got into the car. Julia never mentioned talking in her sleep the night before. I don't think she had any idea that she'd done it.

Driving was even easier for me that morning than the day before. On the way, Julia wanted to know why Alvin and Marcus hated each other. I couldn't think of a great answer. All I could remember was this one time when our Uncle Ruby hired this old woman to teach us Italian. Alvin and Marcus and I would sit around with her all day trying to read these really colorful Italian magazines, and the old woman would never give us any help at all, because she said the language would come more naturally if we discovered it ourselves. After a few weeks we realized she didn't speak any Italian at all. Alvin really loved that. That's exactly the kind of thing that made Alvin really happy. But Marcus had a huge problem with it, and said something to our uncle. When our Italian teacher ended up getting fired, Alvin was so mad he wouldn't talk to Marcus for a year. I was surprised when the whole story came back to me right there in the car with Julia, because I hadn't thought about it since.

"But how long ago was this?" she asked.

"We were just a bunch of tiny little kids."

"And that's it? That's the reason they still don't get along?"

"I think that's one of the reasons. I guess you can ask him yourself."

All the apartment buildings in Sherman Oaks looked basically the same to me, with the iron fences and the same community swimming pool, and even after a year it sometimes took me a second to remember which one I lived in. Outside, I noticed that the dumpster was filled with piles of clothes, and a chair, and the smashed pieces of a dresser, and a bunch of shoes, and a pretty good rock collection, and some basketball posters. It all belonged to me. Marcus had thrown all my stuff away.

I rang the doorbell a few times before Marcus came to the door in nothing but a towel. He had shaving cream all over his chest.

"Hi Marcus." I tried to smile at him, but he wouldn't even look at me. "Julia, this is my brother Marcus."

"Really nice to meet you." Julia beamed at him and offered her hand. Marcus wasn't in a friendly mood, but he shook it anyway.

"You called here yesterday," he said.

"That's right."

"You're Alvin's girlfriend."

"I used to be. But that's not why I'm here." Julia giggled. For some reason meeting Marcus was making her act very young. "Joe said maybe I could use your computer. I'm going to see if I can find an earlier flight."

"But Joe doesn't live here anymore. How could he be inviting over any guests?"

"Please don't be mad at him. I made him stay out late yesterday because I was scared to be alone. But he was worried about you the whole time. He didn't want to let you down."

Marcus crossed his arms and looked at me for the first time. "What happened? Did your big plan with Alvin fall through?"

"How was your game last night, Marcus?" I asked.

"Hotly contested. But we managed to squeeze out a three-point victory."

"I bet you scored a million points."

"I grabbed a crucial rebound in the closing seconds."

"That's pretty great. Should we all go in now?"

Marcus turned to Julia. "Joe thinks that four seconds of flattering small talk can wipe away the unbelievable disrespect he shows for all my hospitality. He believes he has some natural-born right to live rent-free in my apartment while disregarding everything I say. But he doesn't realize that this time it's too late. I've already started to convert his room into a private gymnasium."

"It doesn't matter," I said. "I can sleep anywhere."

"Why should I, Joe?"

"Are you serious?" said Julia. "Where is he supposed to sleep?"

"He should have thought of that when he ran away yesterday."

"You're going to turn away your own brother?"

"I seriously doubt that you have any conception of Joe's unbelievable disrespect for everyone around him. I stated my ultimatum very clearly, and he decided to ignore it."

Julia just smiled back at Marcus as he kept talking at her in this very mean and superior way. Then I saw him get an idea. He turned to me and smirked. "All right, I'll tell you what. If you play basketball with me, right now, then you can move back in."

"Right now?" Playing basketball with Marcus was about the last thing I felt like doing, but I also didn't feel like sleeping in the street that night. He was pretty excited when I agreed. I think he'd really been practicing a lot.

"If I detect anything less than the maximum effort from you, the agreement is void."

He opened the door and we followed him inside, where all these weights and building tools and lumber were stacked all over the place.

"I must have known what a softie I'd be—how easily I'd fold—because I haven't thrown away your bed yet. No matter how harshly I'm punished for my sense of family obligation, I just can't seem to get rid of it." He turned to Julia. "Basic manners dictate an invitation to join us for dinner, but this basketball game may take a while. You may use the computer in the kitchen while you wait. We also have an excellent collection of DVDs or, if you prefer to read, you will find the bookshelves filled with fascinating and informative books. Help yourself to any beverage from my refrigerator. You will find them all powerfully chilled."

"You're so funny," said Julia. "You're not like Joe or Alvin. How can three brothers turn out so differently? Is your middle name Lou?"

"No, why?"

"I just think Marcus Lou would be a really good name for you. Why do you shave your chest?"

"What?"

"You have shaving cream on your chest."

Marcus looked down and wiped some of the shaving cream off. "It makes me feel clean. Are you going to wait here?"

"Maybe I could take a little nap."

"Feel free to nap on the living room sofa. And of course you'll stay out of any room I didn't specifically mention."

"Good luck," said Julia.

Julia took a nap on the sofa while Marcus and I went down to this huge park we had three blocks away. Along with basketball they also had a bunch of baseball diamonds, and some grass and tennis courts and picnic tables and some trees. There was a very angry full-court game happening on one of the basketball courts, but the other one was empty, so that's where we played. The paint lines were worn down and the nets were all torn off, but the rims were good and always pretty friendly to me. Marcus's uniform was so shiny that I could almost see my reflection in his shorts. I played in the clothes I had on.

I could do basically anything I wanted on a basketball court, because this one time I did nothing but play basketball for fifteen years, and so I got extremely good. That day in the park I fell in love with the rim right away. I made almost all of my shots while Marcus made us play best out of three, and then best out of five, and then best out of seven. Even after it got dark and we were playing in the lights from the tennis courts, and everybody else had gone home, he only quit because he got so angry that he kicked the ball way over onto one of the baseball diamonds, where some kids picked it up and ran away with it.

"These rims are virtually unplayable," he told me as we were walking home. And then, "You know, she's not really that pretty."

"What?"

"Julia. With that birthmark on her neck? For Alvin to fall that hard for a girl, you'd think she would be perfect."

I hadn't noticed any birthmark on Julia's neck, but when we got back I saw that Marcus was right. It was right below her ear, about halfway up her neck, maybe the size of a kernel of corn. But I still couldn't understand what Marcus was talking about. It's not like she would have been any prettier without that birthmark.

She'd gone shopping after her nap, and was cooking cheeseburgers in the kitchen when we got back. The apartment was warm and smelled like dinner. Marcus had me scoop some avocados while he took a shower, and then he mashed together a bunch of guacamole in a bowl.

"This was a great breakthrough," he told Julia. "We didn't discover until Joe was fourteen that he would eat guacamole, as long as it was on a cheeseburger."

"I love it," I admitted.

We sat around on the living room couches and ate the cheeseburgers and guacamole off plastic trays. Marcus told a long story about the bus breaking down on the way to his summer league game, but I can't remember any of it. Then as he was finishing up his beer, he asked Julia how Alvin had been wasting all his time in Tennessee. I don't think she liked the question, and for a second I thought she might throw her plate at him or something, but instead she just kicked off her shoes. I can remember being surprised by how tough and strong her feet looked, like she'd been walking barefoot on a mountain. Her feet looked so much tougher than she did.

"He had a full-time job, for your information," she said.

"That's pretty hard to believe," said Marcus.

"He worked every day from eight to four, and sometimes longer."

"Okay. But did he eventually get fired?"

"It just didn't work out."

"I guess that means he did." Marcus laughed, and opened another beer, and offered one to her too.

"What makes you think I drink beer?"

"I thought all the kids drank beer these days."

"They do?" Julia turned to me. "You drink beer, Joe?"

"I hate the taste of beer."

"It makes no difference to me if you drink a beer," said Marcus to Julia. "I was only offering it as a friendly gesture."

"Oh. In that case, I guess I can drink one beer."

Julia took the beer and gave Marcus a little toast before she took a sip. I thought the beer was Marcus's nice way of telling her that he was done insulting Alvin, but it turned out he was only getting started.

"So what went wrong with Alvin's employment situation?" he asked. "Did he turn out to be totally irresponsible? Did he make a bunch of promises he didn't keep?"

"I told you. It just didn't work out."

"Is that also why you two broke up?"

"I have an idea," said Julia. "Why don't we talk about your love life for a little while? Then we can move on to mine."

"No, my love life isn't interesting at all. I don't have Alvin's smoldering good looks and dangerous flair. I don't leave a trail of drama and destruction everywhere I go."

"What's your problem with him, anyway?"

"With Alvin?" Marcus seemed surprised. "He didn't tell you?"

"No."

"I guess that's not surprising. I doubt meaningful communication was a huge part of your relationship. Do you even know what happened to our parents?"

"Yes."

"What did he tell you? That they're stuck in North Korea? That they became political prisoners?"

"Yes."

Marcus just laughed. He never believed our parents had been kidnapped in the Pacific. He thought Alvin had made the whole thing up, and they'd actually been killed in a car crash on Hollywood Boulevard. He didn't even think our parents had been secret diplomats. But I guess he didn't feel like arguing about it right now.

"Did he tell you who raised us?"

"Uncle Ruby."

"Uncle Ruby?" Marcus laughed again, louder this time, and I think he might have burped right in the middle of it, because I could smell the beer in his breath all the way across the coffee table. "Uncle Ruby was an old college buddy of my father's. He signed the necessary papers to keep us out of foster homes, but he lived on the East Coast most of the year. Uncle Ruby never raised anyone. We raised ourselves. Didn't you ever wonder why Alvin didn't need to go to high school while he wasted all that time in Tennessee?"

"He was taking a year off."

"Is that what he told you? When do you think was the last time he went to school?"

"It's not like I spent all my time interrogating him."

"He didn't tell you that either." Marcus was so happy now. "Sounds like you guys had an incredible connection." Now he turned to me. "When was the last time Alvin went to high school, Joe?"

"I can't remember." Whatever Marcus was trying to do, I wasn't going to help him by answering any questions.

"Should I give you a hint?"

"Pretty early on," I said. "Towards the beginning, I guess."

"He dropped out in his first week of freshman year," said Marcus. "And why was that, Joe?"

"You know why."

"But I want to see if you remember. What was Alvin's big idea that couldn't wait?"

"He was building a washing machine."

"Don't sell it short. It wasn't just any washing machine."

"Alvin invented a machine that washes and dries all in the same compartment," I explained to Julia. "That way you don't have to move your clothes from one machine to another. But it was pretty hard to make it work, I guess, and after a few years he met you, so he never quite finished it."

"I think that's a really good idea," said Julia.

"It's a terrible idea," said Marcus. "It already exists, for one thing, and it's more expensive than the two machines it replaces. Any space-saving value is negated by its horrible noise and inferior performance."

"Maybe he thought he could do it better," said Julia.

"He never had any intention of finishing it. The whole project was just an excuse to skip out on his education. He just thought it was funny to find the least productive way to spend his time."

"And that's why you hate him? Because he quit high school for a reason you don't like? What did he ever do to you?"

"It's not what he did to me." Marcus leaned happily back in his chair and slowly took another sip of beer. I started thinking of reasons to leave, because I knew what was coming now. This was Marcus's favorite topic. "It's what he did to Joe."

"What are you talking about?"

"You're unbelievable," said Marcus. "You literally don't know anything. You could at least make the argument that Alvin was too smart for formal education, and so it was a good decision for him to blow off school and live on his wits. But it was certainly a terrible idea for Joe. Joe never scored as a genius on any test. And whatever Alvin's brain got, Joe got the opposite."

"Hold on." Julia turned to me. "You dropped out of school too?"

"I'm studying for my GED right now."

"Alvin was so smart growing up that nobody appreciated

how slow Joe was," said Marcus. "He had terrible problems learning and retaining information and no concentration at all. He couldn't listen. He was constantly distracted and couldn't focus on anything long enough to understand it. He didn't process life as it was happening to him. My mother knew he had some kind of attention disorder, at the least, and my father was starting to see it too, and if our parents had been around longer, I think Joe could have muddled his way through. They would have put him on some drugs, some special classes maybe. At least he could have learned to read. I'm sure plenty of kids worse off than Joe have grown up to be functional adults. But Uncle Ruby wasn't any influence at all, and before anybody else could get involved, Alvin took control."

"What do you mean, he took control?"

"With our parents gone, Alvin decided to raise Joe himself. He liked Joe the way he was and saw Joe's mental challenges as a castle to be defended at all costs. I'm still astounded by the passion and energy he put into this project, especially for a boy of eight years old. He made it his life's work to make sure that Joe was never officially diagnosed, never received any help, never changed, never grew up at all. He taught himself to write left-handed so he could do two sets of homework, and he even had a third handwriting for forging doctor's notes. Of course, all this was only possible because our school was so terrible. High school was a lot trickier to pull off, because they weren't in the same classes anymore, and so after two days Alvin decided they should both drop out entirely."

"I think you're messing with me," said Julia.

"Do you know why Joe only eats pizza and cheeseburgers?"

"It's just what he likes. It was a phase that stuck."

"It was Alvin's idea. In third grade Alvin got tired of being so skinny, and decided to only eat pizza and hamburgers for an entire year, to see if he could put on any weight. He didn't want to do the diet by himself, so he convinced Joe to try it too. It didn't work for Alvin, so he gave it up. But Joe couldn't give it up. He's been trapped in that diet ever since."

"That's ridiculous," said Julia.

"You asked me why I hated Alvin. I'm answering your question. It's because he ruined Joe. He'd always liked playing little mind games with his twin brother, making them switch names and so forth, but after we lost our parents it turned into an obsession. He was determined that Joe would never change, and it was impossible to stop him. Anyone who tried to interfere immediately became his enemy. One year I convinced the school psychiatrist to take a look at Joe, and even got him to prescribe some medication. When Alvin found out what I'd done he tried to kill me with rat poison. That's how determined he was. And he always had a special hold over Joe. At a certain point it was just too exhausting to fight him. I had my own life to live."

Marcus looked a little exhausted. He had barely touched his second beer, but he took a long swig now while he got his breath back. I knew he wasn't nearly finished yet.

"I'll give you another example," he said.

I didn't feel like hearing any more examples. I got up to go pee. The hallway to the bathroom was too dark to see, so I had to feel my way along the wall, and I guess Marcus had started some electrical work in there, because when I felt around the doorway for the light switch, there was only an open socket, and so I got a pretty nasty shock. There was a tiny buzzing sound as I stood there with my whole body twitching until I finally yanked my hand away. Then I just stood there in the bathroom in the dark, letting my eyes adjust, while I could still hear Marcus droning on in the living room about how terrible my education was. The bathroom was extremely clean, like everything he does. He told me once that every time he comes in here to use the bathroom he first takes off all his clothes and folds them neatly in a pile, to make sure they won't absorb any smells, and then afterward he takes a shower. I can remember that his enormous gray cat was curled up in the bathtub watching me. As my eyes slowly adjusted, I could see the cat's red eyes staring up at me and Marcus's basketball team photo hanging over the sink, and I could see Alvin standing by the window.

He was wearing this Hawaiian shirt and a white sailing hat.

"Hi Alvin."

"Are you all right, Joe? You look like you just fainted or something."

"I got electrocuted."

"Listen, Joe. Do I look younger to you now?"

He did seem younger, all rested and tan. He sure looked better than the last time I had seen him.

"Definitely."

"It must be the air and the ocean. The surf. The breeze."

"So you like sailing?"

"It's incredible, Joe. Yesterday we saw three whales swimming in unison along the coastline, just as the sun was setting."

"Will you send me a picture?"

"You know I don't believe in pictures. That's why I'm telling you right now."

"I still wish I could have gone with you."

"No, you have to get past that. You have to start thinking of a way out of this prison. If you stay here Marcus is going to make your life a living hell. He'll ruin you, Joe, and you know it."

"Where else can I go?"

Alvin thought that over for a while. The cat was sitting in the sink now, staring at me.

"Why not Tennessee?"

"Really?"

"It seemed like an easy place to survive, when I was there. You already know one person who lives there. You can leave the dog with Marcus. It'll be easier than taking care of you, so that makes it a good deal for him too, doesn't it?"

"I guess when you look at it that way."

"You have to get out of this apartment somehow." He looked around at the bathroom and shivered. "This place gives me the creeps."

I went over to the doorway and listened to see if Marcus was still talking about me.

"Joe was Alvin's masterpiece," he was saying. "A practical joke that has gone on for eighteen years. He created this impossible person who's incapable of accumulating experience, and who can't make any sense of anything that happens to him."

I decided I didn't want Julia to hear any more of this. When I looked back into the bathroom, Alvin was already gone. My body still felt tingly as I went over and peed in the toilet. When I went back into the living room, Marcus smiled up at me, like he hadn't spent the last twenty minutes talking about how dumb I was. Julia made room for me on the couch, and I remember that she put her hand on my shoulder when I sat down.

"Our parents left us all a little bit of money," said Marcus. "I set up an account for Joe, and he's allowed to take out up to a hundred dollars every day. I think he gambles most of it. Soon it'll run out, and then he'll be forced to make some contact with economic reality, but probably not much. He's got a strange knack for survival. He seems to find friendship and shelter wherever he goes. People like Joe. It's easy to make him happy and he won't ask you embarrassing questions. He buys what you're selling. He doesn't care what it is, or where you got it. And a friendship with Joe is like a badge of open-mindedness. Sometimes I catch myself showing him off, giving outrageous facts about him in a casual way, as if his situation weren't strange to me. Just knowing him makes a person seem automatically more interesting. It's like owning an exotic turtle. And he really is just like a small, blind turtle. He just crawls in whatever direction you point him."

"What's wrong with that?" said Julia.

"What's wrong is that it's tragic," said Marcus. "I'll give you one last example. While you were napping, Joe and I went down to the Riverside court for a few games of one-on-one basketball. He beat me soundly, almost effortlessly, and it was embarrassing and sad for both of us. Sad for me because I'm a NCAA scholarship athlete, and today I was exposed as a player of extremely limited abilities. But it was even sadder for Joe, because he exposed himself as something much, much worse. A player of unlimited abilities with nothing in the world to show for them. Such incredible potential, squandered for Alvin's entertainment."

"So I guess you must be pretty perfect," said Julia. "What have you done with yourself that's so special?"

"I'm glad you asked," said Marcus. "With nothing but hard work, I've turned my mediocre basketball talents into a free college education. I'm finishing up a major in economics, with a double minor in Spanish and Chinese. Think about the fact that Spanish could be a majority language in this country within twenty-five years, that on this planet one out of every five of us is Chinese. Think about markets for a moment. Think what my skills will be worth to an expanding company."

This is how I remember Marcus when I think about him, perched on the couch with his empty second beer, sweat beading on his nose, lecturing Julia so passionately.

"I'm not beautiful like my brothers," he said. "And I don't have any amazing gifts. But the turning point of my life was realizing how little talent is worth. That the qualities I'd always thought to be my faults, my plodding nature, my narrow-minded focus, my constant preoccupation with the future, were actually my greatest gifts, the secrets to realizing all my goals. It was so exhilarating when this finally dawned on me. It felt as if I'd memorized a long poem as a child and recited it every day for many years, and then one day discovered that the whole thing rhymed."

Marcus looked at me and smiled. Then he took a handful

of peanuts from the bowl on the coffee table. He cracked
one from its shell and tossed it to me in a high, slow arc. Before I could think, I opened my mouth and caught it. Right
away I wished I hadn't, but I couldn't help myself.

"Amazing," he said. "You're still hungry."

"I don't believe you," said Julia.

"Which part don't you believe?"

"You're telling me Joe can't read?"

"Of course I can read," I said.

"We won't embarrass him by asking him to read something." Marcus laughed and looked at his watch. "I want to
walk off this food before I do my stretching for the night.
You can snooze on the couch until your flight. But Joe's cur-
few will be ten o'clock from now on, so please make sure he
has the dishes done by then."

My bedroom had already changed a lot since the last time I'd
slept there. Marcus had moved all his weights and exercise
machines in there, and one of the walls was halfway painted
black, and the whole room smelled like sawdust for some
reason. I was already tucked into bed when Marcus came in
to say goodnight and to lay out the new rules I'd have to follow if I wanted to keep living there.

"You're going to build your life the same way I built
mine," he said. "By making an aggressive plan and then
sticking with it."

We were going to have mandatory study sessions, and I was going to eat normal food until I liked it, and no more gambling would be allowed at all, and a million other rules I'd never be able to remember. When he finished going through it all, he patted me on the shoulder in this really friendly way and said, "It's good to have you home," but I could tell he wasn't quite ready to leave yet, because he started pacing in these very nervous circles around my bed.

"Listen, Joe," he said. "I'm going to be starting a family sometime in the next ten years, and lately I've been thinking a lot about baby names. I realized that Alexander is really the only name I could ever imagine giving to my firstborn son. I always knew this intuitively, but not consciously, not until recently. If you happened to have a male child before I did, you wouldn't steal my thunder, would you? You wouldn't name him Alexander, knowing what that name means to me?"

"I doubt it."

"I'm afraid I've got to make it another condition of you staying here in my apartment."

"Okay, Marcus. I promise I won't ever name anybody Alexander."

"That's terrific. I'm so glad that's out of my way." He patted my hair again. "Goodnight, Joe. Tomorrow we'll get all your stuff out of the dumpster."

It was good to be back in my bed, I'll admit. Marcus had

thrown away my favorite pillow, but I had packed my good pajamas and my bed still smelled like me. I was starting to drift off to sleep when Julia snuck in. Her palm was cooler than my forehead.

"Are you sleeping?"

"No."

"I don't like how he talks about you."

"Like how?"

"Like there's something wrong with you. I don't believe half of the things that he says, and I like the way you are. Why does everybody have to grow up so fast? Marcus is one of these people who wants everybody to be the same. I think it's pretty funny that he's accusing Alvin of ruining you, when all Alvin wanted to do was let you stay how you were."

"That's what Alvin says."

"He's right about one thing. You're pretty good company. What will happen to you here?"

"I guess Marcus is finally going to whip me into shape." I tried to laugh. Julia was sort of stroking my forehead the whole time we were talking. She would start at my eyebrows and stroke all the way down to the back of my head. I couldn't stop looking at her lips. "Or I could go with you."

"I had the same idea," she said. "I could probably get you a job at the hotel. I'll be working there all summer, up until I leave for college."

"All my clothes are in the dumpster."

"I know it's really bad, but I think you should just leave them. I really think we should just run away."

She helped me find my shoes, and within two minutes we were sneaking out of the house together. Marcus came out of the apartment building in his bathrobe while we were getting into Alvin's car. He didn't seem angry, just very disappointed. I walked over to him to say good-bye.

"Running away again," he said. "I shouldn't be surprised. But for some reason I am. I thought this time would be different."

"I know I can't come back. I'm sorry, Marcus."

Across the street Julia was starting the car. She waved at Marcus. He huddled in his bathrobe and wrapped it tighter around himself.

"How come nobody likes me, Joe? There are a lot of things to like about me. I handle all my responsibilities. Instead, this girl runs off with you. What's wrong with me?"

"I don't know. Good-bye, Marcus."

"Goddamn you, Joe. When are you going to learn to act like a man?" Marcus suddenly got really angry. I had the feeling that he was about to punch me. "I'm so tired of you. Get out of here. Just get the hell out of my sight."

But when I tried to leave he grabbed my arm and pulled me close, and I could feel him spitting on my ear, "One day you're going to realize your actions have consequences.

What will you do then?" Across the street Julia was starting the car. Marcus glared at her. I tried to pull my arm away. "That girl's too complicated. She knows something she's not telling you."

"Good-bye, Marcus," I said. "Good-bye, good-bye, good-bye."

He went inside without looking back at me again. I walked across the street and got into the car. Julia smoothed my hair a little bit and said, "Lights, Joe." I turned on the lights and we drove away from Marcus's house, past the McDonald's and onto Ventura Boulevard.

"Do you know how to get there?"

"East," she said. "We just keep going east."

Julia helped me find our way onto a wide, fast highway, where driving was even easier than on the city streets, and after a while I couldn't taste Los Angeles in the air anymore, and we were cruising through an open desert.

"You'll have to tell me when we reach someplace you've never been," said Julia.

"It's already happened."

"You're so full of surprises. You never mentioned being so good at basketball."

"That's because I'm not a show-off."

"Why don't you do something with it?"

"Like what?"

"I don't know. Like play in college. Or play on a pro

team somewhere."

"I can't play with people yelling at me all the time. I always go on tilt."

"That's like the fourth time I've heard you say that. What does that mean?"

"You play poker. Alvin must have told you what it means."

"He never taught me that word."

That one stumped me for a while. I drove through the dark, empty desert for a pretty long time before I thought of a way to explain it.

"Poker is really hard and it's always impossible to know what you should do," I said finally. "But sometimes, even when you know exactly what to do, you go ahead and do the wrong thing anyway. You bet when you know that you'll probably lose."

"Why would anybody do that?"

"Some people get all drunk, or get angry at the cards, or they start to believe in different kinds of magic. Some people just can't remember they're supposed to be trying to win." This last part was something Marcus was always telling me. "Marcus never goes on tilt."

"What about Alvin?"

"Sometimes. But in a different way."

"What about you?"

"I'm usually on tilt."

"I think I'd like to be on tilt for a while." She rolled her seat way back so she was basically lying down. "We forgot about Max," she said.

"That's okay. Marcus will take care of him, for sure. He loves dogs, and it's easier than taking care of me."

"Listen to us, Joe. Listen to the way we're talking. What would people think if they could hear us? When did my life become totally insane?" Julia bit her arm for a second, like she was trying not to scream. "I just realized I have no idea what I'm doing. Absolutely none."

She closed her eyes and soon I realized that she'd fallen asleep. I drove all night and it was pretty easy except for this one place, climbing over all these mountains that I'd never realized were so close, when I got suddenly a little sad, because I felt like I was falling off a cliff away from Marcus, instead of just driving away from him. I wasn't waiting for Alvin to come home anymore. I was off on my own. Even now, remembering that night, it still makes my chest thump to think of riding off like that with Julia in the dark. Alvin and Marcus were the only two people I'd known my whole life, and I had no idea when I'd see either one of them again.

Julia was sleeping and the sun was rising when the car suddenly broke so badly that I couldn't drive it anymore. I had to pull off the road next to a whole bunch of corn growing next to the highway. Julia woke up pretty quickly.

"What's happening?"

"The car's broken."

She rubbed her face and looked around.

"Do we have a flat?"

"I don't know. It just stopped working."

She leaned over and looked at the dashboard. "The car's not broken. You just ran out of gas."

"What?"

"You didn't see the light?"

"What light?"

"Are you really not familiar with the gas light?"

I started to go on a very nervous kind of tilt. I felt like I was back at school, and that some teacher was asking me to read something impossible. I had never driven a car long enough to run out of gas before.

"I guess I just missed it."

"You don't know about the gas light?"

Julia squeezed up against the car door like she wanted to be as far away from me as possible. From the way she looked at me, and the way she kept shaking her head out the window, I got this very strong feeling that she didn't want me to come with her to Tennessee anymore, that I'd have to spend the rest of my life in this cornfield, or else go back to Los Angeles and beg Marcus to let me back in his apartment one last time. But then slowly her expression changed. I could see her whole body relax, and now she seemed more curious than anything else.

"How do you do that?" she asked me.

"What?"

"You're so calm. Alvin was never this calm. Were you just born this way?"

"I can't remember."

"The strangest part is that I feel it's actually contagious. It's a nice way to live. You just drive the car until it stops working. You don't even care why. Then you just sit and wait for the next thing to happen."

"You're making fun of me."

"I'm not. I'm really not. In fact, I want you to teach me. And you must have a pretty calming effect on me too, because the old Julia would be totally freaking out right now. I can see why people like you, like Marcus says. You just float along. No matter what happens, you take everything in stride. We're in the middle of a cornfield, totally out of gas, and it barely affects you at all. How do you manage not to stress out about this?"

"I don't even have to think about it."

"I always worry about everything. So what's your secret? How do you handle this situation, for example? Do you start walking to a gas station? Do we wait to get randomly rescued by a stranger? Do we just sit here until we starve to death? Am I asking all the wrong questions?"

"I guess we should start walking," I said.

We got out of the car and walked along the grassy shoulder of the road. About an hour later we finally found a gas station, and I took out some money from an ATM, and bought this little can of gas, and also a Skor bar, and some milk. While we were walking back, Julia asked me, "Is it true what Marcus said? Can you really not read?"

"I could read if I wanted to."

"I promise it doesn't bother me at all. I just want to know. Actually I think it's interesting. I never met anyone our age who couldn't read."

"You should see my signature," I said. "The handwriting is really very good."

"You can't, then."

"Not yet."

"This is so unbelievable. I just have no idea what I'm doing. What on earth is happening to me?" She balled up her fists and screamed silently up at the sky. "I'm getting a crush on a boy who can't read."

It took me a few seconds to realize what Julia had just said. I'd had crushes on other people before, but this crush was on me, and I could feel it washing through my whole body. I can remember how nervous and excited my stomach was, like I was constantly about to burst out laughing. Most of all I felt lucky, like I'd hit an impossible shot, or drawn an impossible card. Everything was different between us from that moment on. For the rest of the day, we switched drivers every few hours, and I watched the gas light carefully at all times. Julia would sort of lean into me once in a while, and it started to feel like we'd been doing this forever.

I found out the country doesn't really change too much as you are driving through it in a car, at least not as much as I thought it would. The restaurants we saw at the end were mostly the same as the ones we saw at the beginning, and I was happy to find out there was going to be a McDonald's every fifteen miles the whole way. At the first one we stopped at, I asked the manager if she knew Francisco. I just wanted to know if he'd finally kissed Carmen, but I saw that I'd only confused her.

"You're ridiculous," said Julia afterward. "How is she supposed to know who any of those people are? But on the other hand—" She frowned, and started rubbing her temples. "What do I know? I'm no expert. Who am I to judge? Who am I to say McDonald's employees don't all know each other? Maybe there's a huge retreat every year, with bonding activities. There's probably a community online. Do you ever feel like you have two voices in your head, constantly arguing with each other?"

I wasn't sure I even had one voice, but I didn't want Julia to feel like she was going crazy. "Once in a while," I said.

We drove the whole second day without getting to Tennessee. I had no idea it could take so long to drive somewhere. We stopped for gas as it was starting to get dark, and

Julia saw a sign for a place called the C'mon Inn, which she thought was a really good name, so we decided to stop there for the night.

I was starting to find out that every motel in the world was different. The C'mon Inn felt more like a house than either of the motels that I'd seen in Los Angeles. It had a bathtub and a flat-screen TV and little toaster oven, too. We walked to this grocery store about a block away and got a bag of pepperoni and some bagels and some shredded cheese, and then Julia made these little bagel pizzas in the toaster oven. We didn't have any plates in the room, so we ate off one of the bathroom towels while we shared the other as a napkin.

I can remember almost everything about that night. After dinner Julia beat me at poker for a while, and we watched a little TV, an exciting show about some different people who all wanted to be famous chefs, and then we unfolded the sofa bed for me. While Julia went into the bathroom to wash her face, I lay down and tested the bed. I could still feel pieces of metal under the mattress, but it was more comfortable than the last one I'd slept on, or maybe I was just more tired. It took me a few minutes to find my pillows hidden in the closet, and I was fluffing them when Julia came out of the bathroom. She had on the same white shorts as she'd worn the night before, but this time her hair was pulled back in a ponytail, and she was wearing this very shiny lipgloss that smelled like cherry candy. I was pretty sure she had just brushed her teeth in there, but I can remember that she was also chewing gum.

"I really think I'm getting used to you," she said.

"I hope so."

"Okay, goodnight Joe."

Julia came over and gave me a hug. I put my hands on her back and held her against my chest, waiting for her to let go. She didn't let go. This was the fifth time I had touched her, and two of the other times were only handshakes, and this one lasted by far the longest. It felt like an hour. Maybe it was only a few seconds. I have no idea how long it was. Just when I thought she was going to let go, she squeezed me even tighter and said, "I feel so much calmer now."

"That's good."

Suddenly she pulled away, smiling, and turned a little red. Then she blew into my eyes. "Made you blink," she said.

Just as I realized we were about to kiss, we did. Nobody really started it. We just both came closer until it was happening. I think kissing Julia had been on my mind since I'd first seen her in the lobby of Alvin's hotel, but I had no idea what it would feel like and no way to imagine it, because I'd never felt another person's tongue before. Her lips tasted like cherry candy but her mouth was minty. At one point she laughed when I accidentally swallowed her gum. Of all the things I'd tried in my life so far, this was already my favorite. I kissed her for maybe five minutes, and then we lay down on her bed and kept kissing.

"I'm cold," she said. "Warm me up."

We cuddled underneath the covers and I put my face into her chest. Her shirt still smelled like bagel pizzas. She squeezed me again, even harder this time. Then she wriggled out of my arms and started messing with my forehead. "You have a zit."

"Where?"

"Right here."

"What are you doing?"

"Popping it. Hold still like a man."

The zit was right over my eyebrow, and it took her a few seconds to pop it. It hurt a lot more than I thought it would. When it was over she kissed my forehead, and hugged me again.

"We're just keeping each other company," she said.

"I can't believe I kissed you."

"Why not?"

"Because I wanted to so badly."

I was only trying to keep the conversation going while we waited to start kissing again, but right away I knew I'd said something wrong. Julia put on this little worried frown and pushed my chest away.

"We're probably both feeling a little lonely, Joe, but it can't mean anything, okay? You have to promise."

"I promise."

"You can't like me too much."

"I won't."

"Kissing isn't supposed to be a big deal anyway. Ginger and I had a kissing competition when she came with my family to Quebec last summer. I kissed nine boys, and Ginger kissed thirteen. It's not like we fell in love with all those boys. How many girls have you kissed before me?"

"Two."

"Come on."

"It's true."

"I don't believe you."

I hadn't thought about either one of those girls for a pretty long time, but I could still picture them both pretty well. "I kissed the first girl on the school bus in eighth grade. I kissed her on the lips, but only for a second. The second girl sold ice cream at the basketball court about three years ago. She really liked Alvin, but she tried to get his attention by pretending to like me. I only ever kissed her on the cheek. Anyway, I wish I'd never kissed either one of them."

"Why?"

"Because then this would be my first time kissing anyone."

Julia's whole body went a little stiff, and again I knew I'd made a terrible mistake. She didn't push me off the bed or anything, but I could tell she sort of wanted to.

"We should probably get to sleep," she said. "We have

another long day of driving tomorrow."

"Okay."

"I'll sleep on the sofa bed tonight."

"I was just talking," I said. "I don't even know what I said."

"I'm sorry, Joe. I just can't be falling in love with any boys right now."

"I take everything back."

"We should probably go to sleep now."

It didn't matter what I said. Julia was starting to climb out of the bed, but I stopped her and took the sofa bed myself. And just like the night before, it took me forever to get to sleep. All night there were planes zooming over our hotel room as I thought about where I'd gone wrong. I was still awake an hour later when Julia sat up in her bed with her eyes wide upon, climbing an imaginary ladder. By now I basically knew what to expect.

"There's not going to be enough breakfast," she said. "There never is."

I sat up. "You're just sleeping," I said, even though I knew she couldn't hear me. "We already bought all this cereal and fruit. Plus, they have breakfast in the lobby."

She wouldn't look at me. "I'm scared."

"There's nothing to be scared of."

"I'm scared to go to college," she said. And I've been eating too much pizza, and now I'm starting to feel fat."

"We just have to get you back to sleep," I said.

"I used to go jogging every day, but now I can't because of my foot. I've been to so many foot doctors, and they're all full of it."

"What's the problem with your foot?"

"I think I might have another cavity. I noticed it this morning. And I think I might have an allergy to wheat."

"Please," I said. "Just try to relax."

"I don't understand your clothing," she said. "I think your pants are way too big. I hate almost everything I've seen you wear."

I climbed out of bed and went over to her. "Don't you want to lie down again?"

"It's dangerous for you to fall for me," she said. "We come from two different worlds. We're not made for each other."

I sat down on the bed. I knew she couldn't hear me, but I didn't care. "You don't know that," I said. "I could change."

"It ended so badly for Alvin."

"Maybe I'm different."

"I'll have to go back to my real life, and I can't take you with me."

"What can I say? You're not going to hear me."

She wasn't moving anymore, just sitting up against the wall and staring into space.

"Alvin is never coming back," she said.

"Of course he is."

"Tomorrow, when I'm awake, I won't be able to say it. But I know he never went sailing. And I know he's never coming back."

"Where would he go if he didn't go sailing?"

"You must feel it too. You just won't admit it yet." Julia's arms started to move, and then her legs. She was climbing her ladder. "We can't just have toast every single day," she said. "There has to be a real breakfast."

I knew there was no point in asking her any more questions. All I could do was talk to her in an extremely soothing way until she calmed down. "Don't worry," I said. "I'll make it right now. We have everything we need."

Finally Julia closed her eyes, and soon she was sleeping normally again. I climbed back into my sofa bed and listened to her breathing while I remembered the whole day one more time: beating Marcus at basketball, Alvin in his sailing hat, running out of gas with Julia, and then that feeling of dropping off a cliff as I drove away from Los Angeles. I realized that I'd forgotten to tell Francisco that I was moving to Tennessee, or to tell Marcus that Alvin had gone sailing around the world. Just before I fell asleep, it occurred to me that I'd left that apartment forever, and I was a little surprised how sad this made me feel, considering that I didn't live there very long.

CHAPTER FOUR

The next morning we woke up early and I drove for half a day. We stopped for lunch just one more time, and then Julia took over, and I fell asleep for a little while, and when I woke up we were in Tennessee. I remember it being a pretty clean city, but not so different from what I was used to, just more people working, eating, talking on their cell phones. The air in the streets smelled a little more like smoke than I was used to, and I saw some cowboy hats and boots, but not as many as I expected, and there was country music playing everywhere.

"Wake up, Joe. We're in Nashville."

We crossed a river on a huge retractable bridge, and passed a football stadium, I think, and then Julia pulled the car into the garage of this enormous department store.

"Where are we going?"

"Have you ever interviewed for a job before?"

"Not recently."

"I did about a million college interviews last year. According to my dad, the way you dress is half the battle. No matter what job you're applying for, he says the secret of an interview is to always wear a suit."

"I don't think I've ever worn a suit."

"Houston will be interviewing you, and he'll definitely feel the same way. He likes manners. He likes to feel like a southern gentleman. Respect is a big deal to him."

"He's your boss?"

"Houston is my brother. I guess he's my boss too. My father is really the boss, but he's having some legal problems, so Houston is in charge of both hotels. He spends most of his time in the city, so I'm running the front desk at Oakwood, until I go to Vanderbilt in the fall."

"What do I need to say to him?"

"Well, I wouldn't mention Alvin, first of all. Houston wasn't Alvin's biggest fan."

"What else?"

"It'll be a piece of cake. He'll notice the suit, and he'll see that you have a good face, and then if he has a job he'll give it to you. And I'm pretty sure he does. Since when do you get nervous?"

It wasn't so much that I wanted a job, but it seemed important to Julia. And if I didn't get one, I thought I might have to go back to Los Angeles, and I wasn't sure when I'd ever see her again.

"It's not like I'm doing it on purpose."

"There's nothing to be worried about, Joe. I'm going to put in a good word for you."

I'd never worn a suit before, but I didn't mind the idea too much, especially since I knew now that Julia hated all my clothes. The men's clothing was on the top floor of this beautiful department store. I must have tried on ten different suits that day, while Julia and the tailor stood around giving me their opinions. I remember that the tailor's hair was always wet but that his skin was very dry. I'd never tried on a suit before, or any nice clothes at all really, so I had no idea how much I would enjoy it. They all had such soft, smooth material, and I loved the way they smelled. The tailor loved most of the suits I put on, but Julia always seemed to find some button or stripe or problem with the fit that ruined almost everything for her. After about an hour they finally settled on this beautiful dark blue suit with very thin white stripes and these amazing, smooth lapels that I could never get tired of rubbing. The tailor said the fabric went nicely with my skin, and Julia agreed, and said it made me stand up straighter, and that I also seemed more mature.

The tailor picked out a dress shirt to go with it, and a

matching blue silk tie, and a couple of pretty nice shoes. After I put on everything, they put me in front of a mirror to see the final effect.

I guess I hadn't been looking in the mirror much, because I'd sort of forgotten what I looked like. My hair was a lot darker than I remembered, and my eyes were a nice dark brown too. I think that suit really did make me look taller, and definitely older, and maybe a little smarter. Compared to the last mirror I had seen, I was pretty happy with what I saw, though I couldn't quite believe it was me.

"Well, what do you think?" asked Julia.

"I love it," I said. "I feel perfect."

"Excellent," said the tailor. He started to help me take the jacket off, but I wasn't having it.

"No, I think I'll just leave it on," I said.

"It's only for the interview," said Julia.

"No. I think I'll just wear it all day long."

"But I have to take it in," said the tailor.

"What?"

"You have to take it off so I can fix it."

I almost strangled him right here, I think. I don't know why, but for a second there I just really didn't want to take off that suit. I got myself together pretty quickly, though, and the tailor marked up the whole thing with chalk before he took it off me. Julia gave him her father's credit card and he told us to come back in an hour.

"Perfect," said Julia. "That's just the right amount of time to get you a nice haircut."

"A haircut?" This was the first I'd heard about this. "Why?"

"We're just going to clean you up a little bit. It's not that I hate the moppy look, but I can barely see your eyes. You have such a high, noble forehead, but you don't let anybody see it."

"I like my hair the way it is."

"It looks a lot like Alvin's haircut."

"So what?"

I could tell she didn't really want to answer me, but finally she did.

"I'm just trying to make sure you get this job," she said finally. "It's not like it's a big deal. I just think you're better off if nobody knows you're Alvin's brother."

"Why?"

"I think it looks strange. My ex-boyfriend is gone less than a week, and here I am recommending his brother for a job."

"You said we don't even look alike."

"There's still a resemblance. Look, I might as well just say it. Alvin wasn't the most popular guy around here. He didn't leave on the best terms. You know how he is. Always messing with people."

This wasn't hard to believe. Most of the people who

knew Alvin were angry at him most of the time.

"I'm just saying, why not make a completely fresh start? Isn't that what you're looking for?"

"Of course." I honestly hadn't thought of it, but now that I heard Julia say it, a fresh start sounded like a good idea.

"You don't want everyone to think of you as Alvin's brother, do you? Don't you want to be known as your own man?"

It wasn't that hard to convince me. An argument will usually work on me no matter what it is. Julia had a lot of good reasons, and the only reason I had was that I liked my hair the way it was. But I wasn't the one who was going to have to look at it.

It turned out to be the shortest haircut I'd ever had, so short that you couldn't even part it, but I had to admit I liked the way it felt. It made my head cooler, and it made me feel lighter and faster. And besides, Julia said she loved it. While they were cutting and washing my hair, she had decided to get her hair dyed to this very light blonde color so I had to wait around a while when I was done. I missed her old hair, and I told her so, but she said this blonde was actually the original color of her hair, and that the fiery red I loved so much had been an artificial dye. It seemed so strange to me, the idea of dyeing your hair back to its original color. She said they matched her natural color pretty well, but not

perfectly, so I guess I never did get to see the real color of
Julia's hair.

I couldn't stop rubbing my head while we picked up my
suit and then got back in the car and left the city behind us.
Soon we were driving down a one-lane road with beautiful forest on both sides. It was getting to be late afternoon
as we turned down a little dirt road that went right through
the forest. We still had to get rid of the car, because it was
the last connection between me and Alvin, so we hid it under
a tarp in the woods and walked the rest of the way on a little
dirt trail through the trees, around a little pond, and then
I think along this old abandoned logging road until we finally arrived at the Oakwood Hotel. It was a big brown
wooden building with a pointed roof, three stories high,
with maybe twenty rooms on every floor. You could tell that
half the building had been a barn a long time ago, because
the wood was so old, but the rest of it looked as new as the
buildings in Los Angeles. There was a huge lawn next to the
gravel parking lot, and this tiny restaurant where nobody
ever seemed to eat, and a swimming pool about the size of
Marcus's apartment. The hotel was surrounded by forest on
all sides, and the whole place smelled like tree sap all the
time.

I guess Houston hadn't arrived yet, so Julia went up-
stairs to her room and left me in the lobby rubbing my new
haircut until he showed up. I was expecting him to look like

Julia, but his skin was much darker. He didn't have any of the little freckles that she had, and his hair was totally black and straight like a horse's. He wasn't wearing any suit—just blue jeans and a short-sleeved collared shirt—but it definitely still felt like he was totally in charge. Being around Houston, you got the feeling that he was the only one who knew exactly how everything worked and how to fix it when it broke. He was used to everybody doing what he said. Later I found out that he'd only been out of college a year, but he was more of an adult than Marcus, because Houston always talked and acted like a man twenty years older than he was. Just like Julia, he'd worked in hotels his entire life.

I made sure my first handshake with him was extremely firm, and I looked straight at his eyeballs while I did it, just like I'd practiced with Julia in the car. Then he took me into this tiny office behind the front desk, where we sat across from each other at a little wooden table with three different phones on it. Before we started talking, Houston just sat there looking at me for a minute. I was already sweating through my suit, because I knew he was looking at my face and that my chances of getting this job probably depended on what he saw there.

"Coffee?"

"I don't really drink it."

"That's good. You're lucky. But I'm going to have a cup."

While he made the coffee, I realized that my hands were

shaking. Houston sat down again with his coffee.

"Where'd you grow up, Joe?"

"I moved around a lot." This was true, although we had only really moved around a lot inside Los Angeles. Julia had helped me memorize a bunch of lies—how I'd moved to Tennessee with my mother, and met Julia in a church—but I didn't want to use them if I didn't have to, because I felt like Houston would know. Luckily he never pushed me very much on where I came from.

"Julia certainly speaks highly of you. She tells me that you're looking for a job."

"That's right."

"Any job in particular?"

"Not really. Just whatever you need me to do."

"Well, I'm not sure if she mentioned it, but our most urgent needs right now are at the swimming pool. Any experience with swimming pools?"

"Just the basics, mostly. But I'd be excited to learn."

"I'm talking about standard maintenance and cleaning duties. You'd also be responsible for the hot tub and the equipment shed, as well as the pool laundry. The job involves some picking up after guests. Are you still interested?"

"Absolutely. Yes."

"Now, for whatever reason, pool men have always been a tricky hire for me. Don't ask me why, but the job tends to attract the worst kind of people. Antisocial and disruptive people. We've had a few terrible pool men. So if you don't mind, I'd like to ask you a couple of questions, just to get to know you a bit. I can't stress enough that none of the questions have right answers, so you can just relax and tell the truth."

"Okay."

Houston took out this pad of paper from the drawer under the table. "What's your biggest weakness?"

I couldn't believe he started with such a tough question. It definitely wasn't one that Julia and I had practiced, and plus I didn't like being interrogated, and I was already starting to go on tilt pretty badly. But just when I was starting to give up on the entire interview, suddenly an answer just came out of me.

"I feel pretty confused almost all the time," I said.

Houston chuckled, and made a little note on his pad. "That's a good one, Joe. Don't we all." I was surprised at how much he seemed to like my answer, because I thought it sounded pretty awful when I said it.

"Are you punctual?"

"Yes."

"Do you drink?"

"No."

"Drugs?"

"What?"

"Are you a loyal man?"

"Yes."

"And what are your ambitions?"

"Ambitions?"

"What are your plans beyond this job?"

"I haven't thought about it."

Again I felt like I'd said the wrong thing, but Houston seemed to like that answer even more than my first one. He was the opposite of Marcus in a way.

"You don't have any plans? You're not looking to move on to something better?"

"No."

"Any interest in college?"

"Not yet."

"How old are you?"

"Eighteen."

"That's nothing to be ashamed of. I was a fine pool man at fifteen, if I do say so myself. Our father made sure we learned every job in the hotel. Did you graduate high school?"

I'm pretty sure Julia had told me to lie about this, but somewhere in there I had decided that I would just tell Houston the truth, because he never reacted the way I thought he would anyway.

"Not quite yet," I said.

"Education isn't important to you at all?"

I shook my head.

"You think you could be happy being a pool man all your life?"

"I don't see why not."

Houston was beaming at me now. He looked like he was having the time of his life. "So far, Joe, you're probably the best candidate for pool man that I've ever interviewed," he said happily. "It's about time someone had some respect for this job. Our last pool man thought he was too good for the position. He couldn't see the dignity in it. But if you look closely, this is the only job in the hotel that's done by a single person, all alone. The pool man takes orders from nobody, and nobody helps him, and nobody notices his work until the day the pool is not perfect. Do you understand what I'm trying to say?"

"Of course."

"I'm looking for someone to lock down this job and make a lifetime out of it. And when you die, we'll bury you under the pool, and your son will fill in the final patch of cement, and then he'll refill the pool and clean it, because he'll be the new pool man."

I could see that Houston was passionate about what he was saying, and I could see it pretty clearly too. I could imagine teaching my son all the secrets of the pool, while Julia stood by with her arms folded, smiling at us in those beautiful white shorts.

"Sounds good to me."

"Can I ask you one more question? Please don't be offended."

"Go ahead."

"Have you ever cleaned a pool before?"

I rubbed my new haircut for a little while before I answered. "I'll be totally honest," I said finally. "I have no experience in any job at all. I'm not trained to do anything. I don't even read well. I've never done anything. Ever."

Houston studied me for a second, like he thought I might be making fun of him, but then his whole face broke into a huge smile. "What a wonderful answer," he said. "Not only does it show exceptional honesty, but I'd actually prefer to have raw and unmolded potential. No bad habits to eliminate. Let's head over to the pool and put you in charge."

"So I passed?"

"That's right."

"I have the job?" I couldn't believe it was happening so fast. I'd never applied for a job before or officially asked for something that I wanted, so I never imagined it could be this easy. "So I have a good face, then?"

"Ha! Julia told you I'd look at your face!" Houston thought that was the best thing in the world. He couldn't stop chuckling about it. "What did she say?"

"Just that you'd be looking at it."

"That's great. That's classic. What else did she say about me?"

"That you'd notice my suit."

"She was right about that. Anything else?"

"I think that's pretty much it. Oh, and she said you were very instinctive."

"Imagine that," said Houston. "She picks up on everything, doesn't she? Yes, I'd say I'm quite instinctive. And for the record, you have a very good face. One of the best I've ever seen."

The sun was already going down, but Houston wanted me to start work the next day, so he showed me the basics of the job that very same night. He taught me how to check the filters and the chlorine levels and the hot tub temperature. The towels were also my problem, and I had to keep the deck chairs in order and fix them once in a while, and I had to clean about a million different things. But it was a good job for me because there was no reading involved.

"People think cleaning a pool is easy, and in a way it is," Houston said. "But it's not the kind of work where you can try to get it over with quickly. You can't finish in half the time by working twice as hard. You have to always be at the pool. If an acorn falls in the pool, a great pool man will fish it out before it starts to sink."

"How long is that?"

"I've timed it actually. It usually takes about thirty seconds for the acorn to sink."

I liked hanging out with Houston right from the beginning. He lived at the hotel in the city but came by to check on Julia a few times a week. He never forgot to come by the pool and say hello. Houston and I turned out to have a lot in common, and gradually we spent more and more time together, and he eventually turned out to be my first good friend.

I took care of that pool for about two months, I guess. From what Alvin had always told me growing up, I figured I'd hate having a job. But it wasn't that hard to keep the pool clean, and swimming in it obviously made people happy. I hadn't ever tried to learn anything but basketball and poker, and those were a long time ago, so I'd forgotten what it felt like to practice something and slowly get better at it. For the first few weeks I focused mainly on the swimming pool. But once Houston saw that I was getting the hang of it, he gradually gave me more and more to do. Eventually I could sweep and make a hotel bed in a pinch, and later I also did some laundry work and learned how to fix certain problems with a toilet. I even spent a little time inside the kitchen when they needed extra help in there.

I slept in the smallest guest room on the second floor of the hotel. It was supposed to be temporary, but I never got around to finding a place of my own, and nobody seemed to care. The hotel was never full anyway. Not even close. We had more than fifty rooms, but we only filled up when there was a big horse race down the road. On those weekends the pool would be totally packed, and everyone would have to work like crazy, and I'd sleep on the couch in Julia's room. She lived at the hotel because her dad lived two hours away, and because she didn't want to live with her mother. She said she wouldn't live with her mother in a million years. She wasn't officially allowed to have boys in her room past midnight, so whenever I slept over I'd have to wake up early and sneak out before anyone saw me.

Julia lived for the summer in this pretty big kitchen suite on the third floor, but it looked more like an apartment than a hotel room. All her old stuffed animals were in there, and the walls were totally covered in photographs—some in fancy frames, others stuck to the wall with double-sided tape. They were full of people that I eventually got to know: Cecily and Granddad, Mr. Manning and Ms. Delancey. I knew most of her family before I ever met them.

Some of the pictures had Julia in them. A few were taken at the hotel, or at her school, or on a river-rafting trip somewhere, but most of her life had happened at this huge wooden country house that I didn't get to see until later. The pictures had been taken over many years, and looking at them was like watching a slideshow of Julia growing up.

You could see that she liked being photographed, because she was always in a pretty good mood, and she never had her eyes closed or a weird expression on her face. As a little girl her hair was bright, bright blonde. It felt strange to see her with a chubby little four-year-old face, because I'd never imagined her ever having been so young. As her hair got a little darker, she got taller and paid more attention to her clothes. She was pretty skinny for a year or two, and later on she got braces, and then broke her leg. Her smile got smaller, then bigger again. She drove a truck and played field hockey. She got a saxophone. A few different boys walked in and out of the pictures, but they never stayed long. I didn't see any pictures of Alvin.

In one picture, Julia was standing next to that beautiful mansion on top of a hill. The picture is taken from a ways down the hill, so you can see just how big the house is, and how small she is against the house, and the forest all around. That was my favorite picture, and the first time I saw it I decided to steal it. I slipped it into the pocket of the suit pants that I wore almost every day by then. That was the first time I'd ever stolen anything where I didn't get the idea from someone else.

I hung out in Julia's room a lot, either watching TV or playing poker. Most of the time we'd end up kissing a little bit, but she would always make us stop. Then she would say it was still too soon after Alvin, and that it felt too strange. This happened over and over again, and I also remember that for the first few weeks she couldn't look straight at me, at least not for very long. If she tried to look into my eyes she'd lose control and get all giggly.

I slept on the sofa when I stayed over, and I would sometimes wake up to find her sitting up in bed, churning her arms and legs and talking in her sleep. She always worried for a minute about breakfast the next morning, who would make it, and what exactly it would be. Once I calmed her down about that, she'd usually go back to sleep, but sometimes she'd stay up and talk to me some more, and it was always very interesting because Julia was a different person while she was sleeping—very calm and unafraid—and she would tell me things she wouldn't normally. That's how I learned her father had almost gone to prison the year before and that her parents had divorced during the trial. That's how I learned she thought her mother had gone crazy.

I saw her mother around a lot, because she came by every week to take Julia to the salon, and sometimes she'd stay and lounge around the hotel in these amazing bikinis. She didn't seem crazy to me, at least not right away. But I didn't get to know her very well, because she never said a word to me or anybody else who worked at the hotel. She was very tall and stylish, with three or four cars and a little truck too. She had long, shining, gold hair and strange, expensive clothes that you would normally only see in a magazine. You could see how Julia came from her, but she was even more beautiful than Julia in a way: more graceful, and more like a queen.

The only time she spoke to me the first month was this

one weekday afternoon when it was absolutely pouring rain. I was in the lobby trying to dry out when she came storming in and demanded that I act as lifeguard while she swam, in case she got hit by lightning and needed to be saved. In all the time she spent around the pool, that was the only time I ever saw Julia's mother swim. She probably did about fifty laps while I shivered on one of the deck chairs and watched. And even though the air was almost as wet as the water that day, I remember that she never let her head dip into the pool and never looked at me again. She just swam her laps in this very slow and smooth breaststroke until the sun came out. Then she left without saying good-bye.

Gradually I met Julia's whole family. Her granddad came by for lunch every Thursday. He was about ninety years old and dressed ten times better than anyone else. It was easy to be around him because he was so polite and hardly ever said anything except, "Well, yeah," in this extremely friendly way.

And she had this little sister named Cecily who would sometimes bring a bunch of her middle school friends to the pool, and they'd spend all day splashing around and giggling. They were always breaking the deck chairs, and so I got to know her pretty well. Cecily was pretty grown-up for her age, but I didn't realize how grown-up she was until one afternoon when I'd been working there about two weeks. I was sitting by the pool in my beautiful new suit when somebody put me in a headlock from behind. I knew it was Cecily when she giggled and twisted my ear so hard that I almost started to cry. She always treated me like I was a doll, and nothing could hurt me.

"Don't think I haven't seen you watching her," she said.

"Watching who?"

"Don't try to deny it. I know you're in love with my sister."

I was pretty impressed that Cecily had figured it out already, since she was only fourteen. But it turned out she had been thinking about me even harder than that.

"How can you tell?"

"Oh please. You only ever sit on this side of the pool, so you can see her walking back and forth from the lobby to the restaurant. You go to the bathroom about ten times more than you should, just so you can pass by her at the front desk. And you always hang around here way after your shift is over, just in case she decides to come out to the pool."

"So what if I do?"

"I knew I was right."

I realized that I didn't care if Cecily knew. It was a relief to talk about it with somebody. "Do you think she knows?"

"It's hard to tell, because she wouldn't admit it if she did."

"What do you think?"

"About what? Your chances?"

"Sure."

"You think I'm a gossip?" Cecily punched me in the stomach as hard as she could, and laughed when I couldn't breathe for a second. "You're right. I totally am a gossip. Okay, I think you might have a chance."

"Really?"

"But only as a summer fling. There's obviously something about you that she likes, but I'm still not sure what it is. You really haven't impressed me too much since you got here, but she needs a nice distraction until she goes to college. And I could see why you'd make a nice rebound guy for her."

"What?"

"She needs a change of pace from her last boyfriend. He was a lot smarter than you, and that's definitely working in your favor. He would always think too much and question everything she did. You don't think about things much, do you, Joe?"

"No. Not that much."

"That's definitely good. That's going to be a couple of points for you. You know our father almost went to jail last year, right?"

"She mentioned that."

"Do you wonder about it? Does that bother you at all?"

"No."

"Good. Because Julia doesn't really need a guy right now

who's going to make her think about all that too much. Also you don't seem moody, so you have that going for you too. But I'd be surprised if you lasted longer than a summer."

"Why?"

"I don't know. Look at you. Every day we break at least one of the deck chairs, and you just fix them every time and never say anything. We're not even guests here."

"So?"

"So you can't let a bunch of middle school girls just walk all over you. If you can't control a simple situation, that's going to be a couple of points against you. Plus you're a pool man, and you obviously can't even swim. That's another point off, for sure. It just doesn't feel right in a girl's mind."

I hated the way this all sounded. Points against me sounded very bad. Cecily was acting like she knew more about me than I did, and suddenly I wanted to ask her a million questions.

"She says I snore in the morning sometimes. Is that a point against me too?"

Cecily shook her head. "Wake up, Joe. These are the least of your problems."

"So what is my problem?"

"You're really asking me?" She thought it over for a little while and finally said, "You're going about it all wrong. You're always hanging around her, trying to make her happy. But what she really wants, she won't tell you. You have to figure it out yourself."

"What's that?"

"She wants the whole package. Our father always tells us how special we are. I know he's just being sweet, but Julia believes him. She thinks she deserves the best."

"Let me ask you something else."

"No way. I'm tired of all these questions."

Cecily giggled. Then she kicked me in the shins, and ran over to the hot tub, where some of her friends were trying to drown each other. They stayed most of the afternoon, and it was starting to get dark by the time I finished cleaning up after them. Every night after I scrubbed down the deck chairs, I liked to arrange them all in a perfect square around the pool. I'd gotten so used to doing it that I couldn't go to sleep until I did. I'd always been sort of a sloppy person and never tried to clean my room while I was growing up, but I felt differently about that pool. I always wanted it to be perfect. Sometimes I'd even come down in the middle of the night to check on it.

Houston came out while I was finishing up. He'd been covering the front desk for Julia that day, and I remember that he had an ice pack on his jaw. Houston always had terrible problems with his teeth, but even when he was in pain he always remembered to notice I was working hard.

"Don't wear yourself out, Joe."

"Just finishing up."

"You're doing a hell of a job out here, you know. Every day I feel even better about hiring you."

"Houston?"

"What?"

"I need to ask you something."

"Go ahead."

He sat down in one of the deck chairs and put down his ice pack. I hadn't been planning to ask him anything until just now, but I guess I was still thinking about everything Cecily had said.

"I don't want to get in trouble."

"Why would you?"

"I don't know."

"Go ahead, Joe."

"Do you think a pool man should know how to swim?"

Every time I thought Houston was going to be disappointed by some problem that I had, it only seemed to make him like me more. He went into his chuckling routine, and even got me chuckling a little too. "No, you're not going to get in trouble. You've got guts to mention it to me, but it's clearly posted that we don't provide a lifeguard." He was talking about this sign tacked up by the hot tub, and I nodded like I had just forgotten to read it. "Why? Did no one ever teach you?"

"I just never learned."

"You surprise me every single day, Joe. It's so refreshing to meet a kid your age who can't swim."

"Is it really hard to learn?"

"Never met anybody who couldn't."

"How long would it take?"

"Depends on how long you practice."

"What if I practice every single day?"

"Then I don't know. Maybe a week or two?" He kicked off his shoes. "Should we find out?"

"Really? You would teach me?"

"It can only deepen your understanding of the pool. I'd see it as an investment in your training. How about a lesson now?"

"Right now?"

"Why not? I've got about an hour before we're having dinner with our dad."

This was all moving so much faster than I ever dreamed. Houston went off to his car for his bathing suit, while I changed in the pool shed. We started our lesson right around sunset, and there was a warm wind blowing, and I can remember that the moon was almost full. He showed me a couple of different strokes in the shallow end that night, but since it was my first class we mostly concentrated on basic water treading, just to make sure I wouldn't ever drown while I was trying to learn the other strokes.

By the time Houston had to leave for dinner, I was already starting to get the hang of it. He said I could have another lesson the next day if I wanted.

"Are you sure you don't mind teaching me?"

"Why would I mind?"

"I don't know. You're busy. And it's not like I'm paying you."

Houston thought that was hilarious. "You're the best, Joe. I'll teach you anything you want."

"Really?"

"What do you want to learn?"

"Can I think about it?"

"Sure. Just let me know. And nice work today."

I stayed there in the shallow end, treading water, while Houston went out the gate to the parking lot and drove away. I was still practicing alone a couple of hours later when I noticed Alvin sitting on the diving board looking at me. I'd been totally focused on swimming, so I had no idea how long he'd been there watching me. His captain's hat and his sunglasses were nowhere in sight, and he looked so much younger now that I almost didn't recognize him. His arms were a little too long, and his hair was sticking up everywhere. He looked about fourteen years old, right down to the golden hooded sweatshirt that he always used to wear. It was much too big for him, because it was actually mine. He had taken off his shoes, and his bare feet were dangling in the water.

"Hi, Alvin."

"You seem surprised to see me," he said. "Did you forget about me, Joe?"

"Of course not."

I knew this wasn't quite true. Living at the hotel was so exciting that I hadn't thought about Alvin for a little while. But now I remembered everything Julia had said, that he hadn't gone anywhere, and how he was never coming back.

"Can I ask you something, Alvin?"

"Go ahead. I'm not going to stop you."

"Are you really sailing around the world?"

He waved his legs, splashing the water with his feet, and bounced up and down a little on the diving board. "Why would you ask me that?"

"Because I don't think you are."

"But it's not like you to come to a conclusion. What's gotten into you today?"

"Why are you getting younger every time I see you?"

"So many questions, Joe. Since when do you wonder about anything?"

"How much younger are you going to get?"

"How far back can you remember me?"

"Alvin," I said. "Are you dead?"

"Come on, Joe. It's a beautiful night. Why go into this now?"

"You can tell me if you are. I won't be mad."

"What's the difference if I'm dead or sailing around the world? Don't we have more important things to talk about?"

"I just want to know."

"Oh, all right," he said. "I came here to relax, not to get interrogated. But I'll confess if it's going to put an end to all this pestering. Can we drop this subject now?"

"So I'm never going to see you for real, ever again?"

"We don't have to be so dramatic," he said. "It's not that sad."

"Why not?"

"If I had lived I probably would have gotten old, and had these awful backaches all the time, and an infection in my eye or something. I was lucky to escape the world without ever interacting with the health care industry."

"What's it like to be dead?"

"When a fish gets caught and thrown back in, what does he tell the other fish?"

"A fish?"

"He could never explain what he'd seen. And they wouldn't believe him if he could."

I couldn't make head or tail of anything Alvin was saying. "What are you going to do now?" I asked him.

"Oh, don't worry about me. I can go wherever I want, and I don't have to work, and nobody can tell me what to do. Finally I'm completely free. I'll probably go visit all these places you've never even heard of. I may just go sailing around the world after all. If I feel like it, that is."

"But you'll keep coming back to talk to me."

"Oh sure. When I have time. Now will you take a look up at the sky? In Los Angeles you could never see the stars this well."

The sky was incredibly clear that night, and Alvin pointed up at some different groups of stars and told me what they were supposed to be. I can remember some of them were supposed to be a dragon, and the other ones I can't remember.

"I just tried to lecture you on outer space," he said. "So I must be twelve or thirteen years old. That's the age where a boy reads a general-interest physics book, and then can give himself a fever just by pondering how small he is compared to the findings of science. The sheer intensity of my dreams and ambitions at this age was sometimes enough to make me cry."

"Are you going to cry now?"

"No, because then you'll start crying too."

"I don't mind, if you need to."

"I won't put you through it. I'll spare you." A cloud blew over us. Alvin sighed up toward where the stars had been. "How long has it been since I died?"

"Just a few weeks, I guess."

"Everyone should be allowed to try out this sensation. You keep the perspective of the age you died, but you feel what it's like to be younger again." He rubbed his cheeks and made a painful face. "Shaving was so horrible. I'm so glad that's over forever, and I've also noticed that my eyesight is a little better now. I can read the pool safety instructions all the way from here. Do you remember anything about this age?"

"Not at the moment."

"I treated you like a dog," he said. "Why did you stand for it?"

"I don't know. It must not have bothered me too much, I guess."

"I only keep harping on it because it's the worst thing I've ever done. But now we should be focusing on you. What are you doing out here? It's not like you to be splashing around in a pool."

"Houston is teaching me."

"That's pretty nice of him."

"We're getting to be friends."

"Good for you, Joe. Anyone is lucky to have even one friend, not that I ever did. Whose incredible suit is slung over that chair?"

"That's mine. I got it for my interview."

"That is so excellent. Nothing says more about you than a properly fitted suit. This is such an important concept. But you've never worn a suit before. What's going on, Joe?"

"It's sort of a secret. Should I really tell you?"

"You should tell me immediately."

"All right. I fell in love."

"That's terrific. You fell in love with Julia?"

"Yes."

"Good for you, Joe. That is beautiful news."

"You're not angry?"

"What a ridiculous question," said Alvin. "You clearly don't understand my firm position on this matter." He climbed to his feet, and stood on the edge of the diving board, looking down on me as he bounced up and down. He spread his arms. He really looked quite special towering over me, with the clouds rushing over him and the stars shining behind the clouds. "I've always maintained that everyone should have the chance to fall in love with Julia once before they die. That idea has always been the center of my personal philosophy." He let his arms fall to his sides. "If I were still alive, I probably would wish that you would get the flu or something, but look at me now. How can I object? She has the softest tummy. How can I possibly fault you?"

"I thought you might be angry."

"Once you've seen her face all rumpled from her pillow in the morning, nobody would stand a chance. That's practically a scientific fact. Don't you love how she sings in the shower?"

It turned out that I hated to hear Alvin talking about Julia. I started to go a little bit on tilt, and for a second I thought about pulling him down off the diving board just to make him stop, but I calmed down pretty quickly. Now he stood up on his tiptoes and starting bouncing up and down even more, looking down into the water.

"This used to be my job," he said.

"You were the last pool man?"

"You knew that."

"I did?"

"Why else would the job be suddenly available?" He bent his knees and bounced a little higher. "Can't say I ever got the hang of it though. Not like you have."

"So you're the one that Houston hated."

"He mentioned that?"

"What did you do?"

"Well, he's your friend, isn't he? You should ask him."

"Maybe I will."

"Does she still get a cramp in her foot sometimes, when she's in bed?" he asked. "Does she have to get up and hop all around?"

"Maybe."

"Does she still turn the TV off when the movie gets too scary?"

"Why do we have to talk about her?"

"Why shouldn't we?"

"I don't know. I don't like it."

"But I just gave you my blessing. I told you. I'm out of

the picture." Alvin bounced one more time and then jumped high off the board, turned in midair, dove into the pool, and disappeared.

The wind was less comforting now, and I was starting to get cold. I didn't feel like practicing my swimming anymore. I went up to my room and took a shower. While I was drying off, my cell phone rang. I'd been leaving it on in case Alvin called me from a sailboat somewhere. I guess I should have known by now it couldn't possibly be him, but I answered anyway. It turned out to be Marcus. I had no idea that he had my number. He didn't even bother to say hello.

"I don't care where you are," he said, "and I'm certainly not worried about you. My life has improved dramatically since you left. The extra free time has made me twice as productive; I'm already feeling the effects of the new gym in my power and explosiveness. So the last thing I would do is try to convince you to come back here."

"How are you, Marcus?"

"Don't try to turn this into a friendly call. I'm only contacting you to give you a very specific piece of information. The dog you so irresponsibly left here has unfortunately been killed running across a busy highway. He was chasing a helicopter flying three hundred feet above him. I'll admit the loss affected me more than I expected. But I certainly can't take any responsibility, given that the care of this dog was never my choice. Anyway, I'm sorry, Joe."

I remembered Alvin's dog a little bit: that neat little poop he had done in the motel bathroom, how cold his nose was, and how he'd licked the manager's hand.

"He was a good dog," I said.

"I'd been calling him Augustus," said Marcus. "That's the name I always wished I had. Well, I don't expect that we'll talk anytime soon."

"I have a job now."

"That seems hard to believe. Good-bye, Joe."

"I have some news about Alvin."

There was a pause. I heard the blender in the background, and I could picture Marcus perfectly, mixing up a drink in the kitchen with his basketball shoes on.

"Why do you think I should care?"

"It's pretty important news."

"Then go ahead."

"I'll give you three guesses," I said.

"If you're going to tell me, tell me."

"Just guess."

"Did he take off with your bank card?"

"No." I already hated this game. I wished I'd never made it up. "Just think of the worst thing that could have happened to him."

I could tell Marcus was getting really annoyed. "Just forget it. Good luck, Joe, wherever you are. Where did you say you were?" I started to tell him, but then he interrupted me.

"Never mind. I don't care." And then he hung up.

I was just about to go to sleep when Julia finally came home from dinner in this long green car I'd never seen before. Houston was driving. The man in the passenger seat I'd never met, but I knew this was Julia's father. He looked older and weaker than he did in her photographs. He was all hunched over in this tattered coat that looked like it was made for a much bigger guy. I knew he'd broken his back falling off a horse one time, and as he climbed out of the car I could see that his spine was crooked. All the way from the window, Mr. Manning seemed sad. I wanted to help him fix whatever was bothering him so much; but even though I'd heard a little about his trial, I had no idea, really, what his problems were.

After Julia kissed him good-bye, she went inside, and Mr. Manning stuck around to help Houston feed the turkeys. The woods around the hotel were full of turkeys, and Houston liked to feed them on quiet nights when he happened to be around. I'd helped him a couple of times, though I didn't really like it. The turkeys ate the food right out of my hand, and I was always sure their beaks were going to cut my palm.

Houston came out with the feedbag and this other little suitcase, and I watched them shuffling across the lawn right underneath my window. They stood at the edge of the lawn, peering into the trees. The moon was very bright, and the forest was so quiet that every turkey in there must have heard Houston rattling his feedbag from a mile away.

Soon I saw the first big turkey come waddling out of the woods, bobbing his head. "Look how he comes to you," said Mr. Manning.

A couple of even more colorful turkeys had already appeared. They had the same loose, disgusting chins. Soon they were fighting over the food in Houston's hand. It was hard to believe they weren't cutting up his hand with their beaks, but they obviously weren't, because he just kept chatting with his father while they ate. Those turkeys couldn't get enough. Houston refilled his hand a couple of times, and then Mr. Manning gave out a couple of handfuls of his own. Then he took the suitcase from Houston, put it in his car, and drove off. Houston went inside to put away the feedbag before he left in his own car.

CHAPTER FIVE

I think it was just a few days later that Houston took me into the city for some pool supplies. We bought a bunch of chlorine and filters and some chair covers, and then Houston spent an hour at the dentist while I sat in the waiting room. Afterward we drove around downtown a little bit and stopped at McDonald's for lunch. Their food wasn't quite as hot as Francisco made it in Los Angeles, but it was pretty decent. I was finishing up my cheeseburger and starting in on the Big Mac when I remembered Alvin's suggestion the night before, and I decided to ask Houston what was so bad about the last pool man he had hired. I tried to do it as casually as I could.

"I fired him for his incompetence," explained Houston.

"He couldn't get to work on time. If he didn't think I'd be around, he had a bad habit of dozing off and sleeping half the day. Just didn't respect the job. I know for a fact that he robbed me at least once."

"So you hated him."

"Who said I hated him?"

"I can't remember. I think maybe Julia did."

I felt like I'd done too much talking already. I knew I needed to stay calm. Houston took a sip of Coke, and I could feel him looking at me pretty carefully. For a second I was sure I'd given everything away. The last thing I needed was for Houston to figure out that I was Alvin's brother, now that everything was going so well for me at the hotel.

"It's true that I disliked him personally as well," said Houston finally. "I'll tell you why, if you really want to know."

"I was just wondering. It doesn't even matter."

"But can I trust you, Joe? Because Julia doesn't really know a lot of this."

"Of course."

"You know they dated, I assume."

I just nodded. I was afraid to say anything out loud now.

"But this guy was nothing like you, Joe. He was a weird person, a loner. He couldn't quite fit in anywhere, and so he didn't want Julia to fit in either. He was always whispering weird ideas in her ear, making her doubt herself and the people around her. He tried to turn her against her own family. Her own father."

Talking about Alvin seemed to be making Houston angry. He'd ordered this chicken sandwich but he wasn't touching it now, just stabbing it with his finger. His voice was quieter now but also more intense.

"As you probably know, my father had some legal problems last year. Bill Manning is a great businessman and he's made a lot of money in this town, and so a lot of people are jealous of him. He had to waste a year fighting a bunch of trumped-up criminal charges. Extortion, money laundering, bribery—they were always changing because none of them had any real foundation. It was as if the prosecution couldn't decide which lies to tell. You follow the news?"

"When I have time."

"The whole thing was just a waste of good taxpayer money, but it was a rough year for my father. My mother left him in the scandal. His bank accounts were frozen. Many of his business contacts got scared off. The last thing he needs is for his own pool man trying to turn his daughter against him too. We're talking about a kid with no respect for family or community. No sense of loyalty. It just made me very angry to see it. Because I know what kind of man my father is. Did Julia tell you how I came to be adopted?"

"What?"

I had no idea that Houston was adopted, and it was too

late now to pretend that I did, because now he had seen it in my face and burst out laughing. "You're amazing," he said. "You just take everything the way it comes. You never wondered why I look different from my sisters?"

"I never thought about it."

"My father was Cherokee. Or at least that's what he told everyone. I always suspected that he came from somewhere in South America, maybe Peru, but thought claiming to be Cherokee made him more interesting. He was a con man and a compulsive liar and a gambler. He had no self-control and had to gamble higher and higher, and when I was five he lost me in a poker game. Not that he knew it at the time."

The man sitting behind me bumped into my chair as he stood up. He threw away his paper as he left, and now Houston and I were alone in the McDonald's. He made a fist and held it out in front of him, looking at it carefully. I could tell the story was important to him and so I listened as hard as I could.

"As the story goes, my real father sat down at a no-limit stud game with Bill Manning and lost three hundred thousand dollars in a single night. He'd backed the money with the house my mother left him, but never mentioned that he'd already lost that property, in another game, the week before. So the next day, when it was time to pay his debts, he went out and put a nice, expensive lobster dinner on his credit card, drove out to the Kennewick Bridge, took off his shoes, and jumped off."

Houston took a bite out of his chicken sandwich. I had no idea what to say. I thought about telling Houston that I'd been orphaned too, but I couldn't remember if I had already lied to him about it.

"What was the hand?"

"Mr. Manning had a set of kings."

"And your father?"

"He was bluffing."

"Wow."

"That was the kind of man he was. I was five years old. When Mr. Manning heard what had happened, he felt so terrible that he adopted me. In the end, the only way he could get a male child was to win one in a poker game. That's how the joke goes, anyway."

I couldn't stop imagining how crushed Houston's father must have felt at the end of that hand. I'd made some terrible decisions myself at the poker table, but never more than a hundred dollars in one day. *I hope I never go on tilt that bad*, I thought. *And lose my kid in a poker game. And die.*

"As I grew up I realized that I'd landed with the better man," said Houston. "My father bet something that he didn't have, and then found the cowardly way out. Mr. Manning took responsibility for what he couldn't. Without Mr. Manning, my whole life would have been a crapshoot. The more I learn about the world, the more his generosity astounds me."

Houston leaned in toward me now. I can remember that one of his eyelids was fluttering a little bit, and they were both so wide open that you could see how round his eyeballs were.

"So yes, it upset me to see some self-righteous high school dropout not only passing judgment on him but whispering in Julia's ear and trying to poison her mind too. That punk wanted Julia to cut off contact with her own family—put off school—all to chase some crazy fantasy of sailing all around the world. I could see it happening as soon as he arrived, how he was isolating her—making her strange and distant. I'm not saying that's why I fired him, but it certainly made it easier. And the second I wasn't his boss anymore, I told him exactly what I thought of him, and that he wasn't welcome around the hotel."

It wasn't hard for me to imagine Alvin trying to cut off Julia from everyone she knew, because that's basically what he had done to me. Houston closed his eyes while he took a deep breath. Then he opened the fist in front of him and laid his hand softly on the table.

"Don't worry, Joe. I know you're nothing like that."

"What do you mean?"

"Oh, please. You don't think I know about your little crush?"

"You do?"

"I appreciate that you keep a professional attitude on the job. But I would have noticed even if Cecily hadn't told me." He laughed. "I guess Julia has a thing for pool men."

"I guess so."

"Don't worry. I've got a different feeling about you. I'm totally in favor this time."

"Because of my face?"

"Well, yes, your face, of course." Houston cracked up again. "But that's not all. You seem good for her. I don't see you stressing her out."

"Cecily thinks maybe I could be a summer fling, but that's it."

"Well, Cecily is fourteen. She's probably wrong about a lot of things."

"What do you think?"

"All I know is that I'm rooting for you. I'm just happy to see Julia moving in the right direction again."

Houston smiled at me and for a second I had that sick feeling that I was betraying Alvin for agreeing with him, but I couldn't help it. I knew that Julia was better off with me. I would take better care of her than Alvin could, and whatever else she needed I could learn.

"I decided the next thing I want you to teach me," I said.

"Okay."

"Actually a few things."

"Maybe we'd better take them one at a time."

"I want to learn to like the taste of different things again."

I went on to explain to him my specific problem with food, and how I could only eat pizza and cheeseburgers and the worst, unhealthiest junk food. Houston listened carefully and decided to start attacking the problem then and there, right there in that McDonald's. He cut out about a quarter of a chicken sandwich for me, and gave it to me folded in a napkin.

"Why don't you try a bit of this?"

"I don't usually like chicken."

"Maybe so, but let's put that aside for a second. Let's pretend this is a food you've never even tried before."

It really did look just like a commercial for a McDonald's chicken sandwich, a little bit shiny and everything, with little drops of mayonnaise squeezing out under the bread. I took a little bite. I had no idea what to expect, because it had been a couple of years since I had tried to eat chicken. But maybe I had changed, or maybe chicken had changed, because it really didn't turn out to be that bad. For the first couple of bites I tried not to breathe, but then I realized the taste wasn't even bothering me. It was as if I'd always liked chicken sandwiches, but had just forgotten for about ten years.

"Look at you," said Houston. "You're doing it."

"It's probably easier for me to eat food from McDonald's."

"Maybe so. But it's a start."

That was the beginning for me. I knew it wouldn't be easy, and I knew it would take a long time. But if I could eat that chicken, I could eat anything. Being around Houston made a lot of things seem suddenly possible, and from that day on he always took an interest in the things I ate.

It was incredibly hot by the time we finished lunch. Driving home, we rolled down all the windows because the air conditioning in Houston's car never worked. We were about halfway home when he said, "Julia tells me you play basketball."

"Sometimes I do."

"Well, there's a court not far from here. How about a quick game right now?"

"Against each other? I don't know." Houston and I had been getting along so well, and I was thinking about Marcus and how angry basketball could make him. "I don't like to get too intense when I play."

"Oh, please, that's never been my style. Besides, we'll play on the same team."

I was full of doubts, but Houston really seemed to want to play, so I finally agreed to play a couple of games, and he got off at the next exit, and took us to these courts he knew. Life is so full of impossible things that I don't understand. It turned out that I had nothing to worry about, because Houston turned out to be a wonderful basketball player, the best point guard that I ever played with. He wasn't very fast or strong, but he never tried too hard or dribbled all around like crazy for no reason. He didn't shoot when he was angry, and he didn't hog the ball like it belonged to him. Playing with a good passer is almost like cheating at basketball because almost nobody ever does it. It becomes impossible for the other team to beat you and they can't even figure out why.

A basketball court might be the only place where I can really pay attention perfectly and understand what's going on. If you're playing really well, it's like you're dancing with the people that are trying to defend you. You can move them around and help them find out where to go. But if you get angry, or if you go on tilt and try too hard, the magical plays will never happen.

I felt right away like I'd been playing with Houston all my life, and I fell in love with the rim early on, and it loved me back. I tickled the net all afternoon and we won all our games, and stopped when we got tired. I was too excited and pleased to talk. It was like we'd been practicing all our lives to play with each other. Houston didn't talk either until we were almost back at the hotel.

"You're a hell of a shooter."

"It was a good day."

"Pickup basketball is always a miracle to me," said Houston. "Nowhere else in the world will five strangers meet and immediately—within seconds—start to function as a single whole. We look each other in the eye. Every wolf instantly knows his role in the pack. Before the game even starts we know our leader, our rebounder, our scorer, our knuckle-down defender, our wise encouragement, our sparkplug of infectious energy, our scapegoat, our passer, our hustle, and our soul." Houston was speaking very passionately now and so I tried to pay attention closely. "Take the big redhead, for example. He was our rebounder."

"You were the passer."

"Correct. The black guy was our hustle, and he also had wisdom. That's an unusual combination in one player. The skinny young kid was our knuckle-down defender. Also rare for a youngster to step into that role."

"You were our scorer."

"No. You were our scorer."

"You were our leader and passer."

"That's right."

"The short kid was also our scapegoat."

"Correct."

"And the redhead was also our soul."

"No, you were our soul."

"But I was the scorer."

"You were our scorer, and you were our soul. Whatever team you play on, you're going to be the soul."

It was pretty normal for Houston to tell me things about myself that I couldn't understand. I liked them because they sounded like compliments, even if I was never sure exactly what they meant.

"Do you really think I have a chance with her?" I asked.

"I know you do."

That was the first day I could really imagine a whole future for myself in that hotel. Once Houston taught me everything I needed to learn, he and I would drive around together and solve important problems. Someday we'd even have an office together. A few times a week we'd both report to Mr. Manning, and he would congratulate me, and everyone would see they'd underestimated me, and every night I'd read in bed aloud to Julia as she curled against my chest. I remember all this very well. Sometimes the easiest things to remember are the things you hoped would happen, even if they never did.

"That was a hell of a game today," said Houston, when we pulled up to the hotel.

"I loved it." I opened the door. "Goodnight."

"We'll play again soon."

"Houston?"

"Yes?"

"Would you teach me how to read?"

"Really?" He wanted to laugh for a couple of seconds, but then he saw that I was serious, and became very interested and serious. "That's fascinating," he said. "Never had an employee who couldn't read."

"Do you think it's too late?"

"You really are amazing, Joe. You really are."

"Is it?"

"Too late? Absolutely not. It won't be easy, though."

"I don't care. I'd study all the time. Would you really teach me?"

"I really would," said Houston. "In fact, it would be my pleasure. Nothing's more enjoyable than teaching a student who wants to learn."

"I'm going to be good," I promised. "One of the best."

"Then we can start tomorrow after swimming practice. Good-bye, Joe."

Sometimes when I look back at everything I did while I was in Tennessee, it almost feels like someone else was doing it. I spent all day in a beautiful suit I never would have worn before, with probably the shortest hair I'd had since I was born, and I spent all my free time practicing new skills. Eating turned out to be a lot harder than swimming, and it took me more than a week to move past McDonald's chicken sandwiches, but I felt like I made progress every day. Reading was a thousand times harder than eating; but I still must have picked up something in school—no matter how much Alvin tried to make sure that I didn't—because I always got this really familiar feeling when I tried to do it. It's not like I could read the newspaper or anything, but after a few weeks

I had the basic letters down, and the first word I honestly read was the beautiful signature I'd been practicing so long.

Over those two months I got to know Houston pretty well. I kept looking everywhere for signs that he was Cherokee. I thought he might have a special way of eating, or a very peaceful stare, but I never saw anything like that. This one time we were all having lunch on the patio, when Julia dropped her fork, and Houston caught it before it hit the ground. I have no idea if a Cherokee would even do that, but it's the only thing I ever noticed in all the time I lived there.

He gave me lessons every time he came to visit our hotel, and we also played basketball as much as we could. To cool down we sometimes jogged a couple of times around the park. I've never gone jogging before, but with Houston it seemed like a normal thing to do. I could feel that slowly I was turning into somebody else, and Julia obviously noticed it too. She brought it up one night while we were lying on her bed playing poker, using lima beans for chips.

"There's something different about you, Joe, but I can't tell what it is. Did you lose weight or something?"

"Maybe. We've been playing almost every day, and sometimes jogging too."

"Since when do you go jogging?"

"Houston says it helps to clear the mind."

"Seems like you guys have really hit it off."

"We're getting to be friends."

"He's taken quite a shine to you," she said.

"I hope so."

"Why do you think that is?"

I tried to think it over. Questions like this didn't make me as nervous as they used to.

"He says he feels like he can trust me."

"That's a nice thing to say. Are you going to deal?"

After the poker game we turned on the TV and started watching this movie about some ex-cops hunting for gold in the jungle. About halfway through I put my hand on Julia's waist, and a little while after that we started kissing. We kissed through the whole movie before she made us stop. This was a lot longer than usual, but finally she turned away and punched the bed a couple of times.

"I can't take this anymore," she said.

"What's wrong?"

"I'm really frustrated. I know we can't keep going. But I also don't want to stop. I'm so tired of it."

"But we're not doing anything wrong," I said. "Alvin doesn't care."

"How do you know?"

"Because I'm his brother. I just know."

"Why do you suddenly have all this confidence?"

"You don't like it?"

"That's not what I said. I'm just not used to it."

"I think it's really good for me to have a job."

"Close your eyes for a second."

I closed my eyes and lay still on the bed while she started touching my forehead, my cheekbones, my lips, all the most important parts of my face, like she wanted to make sure they were real. When I opened my eyes I found her staring at me very carefully and almost smiling—but not quite. But the minute she realized that I could see her, she giggled and buried her face in my chest.

"Why can't you ever look at me?" I asked.

"I just was."

"But not when my eyes are open. You always have to look away. You're doing it right now."

"I am not. Watch."

She looked me straight in the eyes for about ten seconds, which was by far the longest that she'd ever done it. I can remember that she held her breath for almost all of it. Then she hugged me again.

"Are you going to stay over?"

"If you want me to."

"But I want to take a shower. You can get under the covers if you want."

Julia jumped off the bed and ran into the bathroom, and soon I heard the shower running. She was probably in there for about twenty minutes. I got under the covers while I waited. I had never slept in her room before when the hotel wasn't full. I already had a feeling about what was about to happen. I guess I had tried to imagine this moment before, based on movies I'd seen or stories I'd heard; but the people that I pictured were always a little different, not exactly me, and not exactly Julia. They looked like us, and acted like us in some ways, but somehow they had more experience, and knew exactly what to do.

When she came out her hair was all wet, and she had changed into this yellow nightgown that hung down over her knees. This is usually how I picture Julia when I think about her, coming out in that nightgown, with the bathroom still all full of steam behind her. I'd seen this look on her face before, when she tiptoed down the stairs into a cold swimming pool. She smelled the same, but stronger, as she got under the covers and put her arms around me.

"I'm cold," she said. "Warm me up."

I rubbed her back and warmed her up as well as I could. "Is that better?"

"Better. Now just hug me as tight as you can."

"I don't want to hurt you."

"I'm stronger than I look. Hug me tighter."

"I am."

"Just a little tighter. One more second."

I hugged her as tight as I could, and when I finally let her go, she was still sort of clinging to me.

"Are you going to take off my nightgown?"

"Okay."

"You don't make a lot of moves, do you, Joe?"

"Nobody ever showed me how."

"You know there are a million reasons why we shouldn't do this."

"I know," I said. "But I can't think of anything at all."

"Should we turn off the lights?"

I got up and flipped off the switch by the door, and the lamp by the bed, and the bathroom lights too. Coming back to the bed, I looked out the window and saw the swimming pool out there, all lit up from below. The deck chairs looked so clean, and they were in a perfect square around the beautiful bright rippling pool, and I knew that there were fifteen lights under the pool because I swam down there and cleaned them every week. I was in charge of the whole thing. And I remember noticing how strange it was to be thinking about those fifteen lights even as I was climbing into bed, and slowly taking off Julia's nightgown, while she started to take off my clothes, too.

Everything from then on happened to me for the very first time. I can remember all her skin, how soft and smooth and delicate it was, but my strongest memory of that first time with Julia is actually the feeling I had afterward, when we were lying on the bed together, staring up at these yellow glowing stars she had stuck to the ceiling. She was lying draped over my chest, and I felt so tired and relaxed and safe. There was nowhere else I wanted to be.

"I love you," I said.

Julia didn't answer, and I noticed she was shaking a little bit.

"Are you crying?"

"I knew I might cry," she said between these soft little sobs. "It's just too much."

"Did I do something wrong?"

"No, I just cry a little bit sometimes. Do you think that's strange?"

"This is my first time."

"No, it isn't."

"It is."

"I sort of wish you'd told me that before."

Julia got up wiping her eyes and went off into the bathroom. I rolled over onto my stomach and lay there with my arm on my forehead, trying to calm down. *I love you.* It had felt so exciting to say it, and I tried it out again, just mouthing the words in the dark. *I love you.* She came back with a big glass of water and tilted it into my mouth until I wasn't thirsty anymore, and then she climbed back into bed.

"Why did you leave?" I asked.

"Can we build a blanket fort?"

"Why?"

"Please? I'll help you."

I didn't feel like it, but we got together all the pillows and blankets in the room, and built a pretty good fort. Then we crawled inside and cuddled for a while in the dark.

"You already know the answer," she said finally.

"How could I possibly know?"

"You know I couldn't let you love me if I didn't love you too."

"I can't understand that."

"When I'm with you I don't think about yesterday and I don't think about tomorrow." She gave me a little kiss on the side of the mouth. "I love you too, Joe."

"You do?" Hearing it felt even better than saying it. "I love you," I told her again.

She laughed. "I love you too, Joe."

"I love you. I love you. I love you!"

That was the best night I'd had so far. We cuddled and kissed and said "I love you" to each other all night long, and when I finally fell asleep I dreamed about kissing her also. It was pretty incredible to dream about the same thing I'd been actually doing, and in the morning we were still in love, and Julia could look at me straight in the face all of Wednesday, and we were in love on Thursday, and on Friday. And on Saturday we took a trip downtown to see a movie about a bunch of rock stars trying to go to high school, and we were in love all Sunday by the pool and that whole night watching basketball and tennis. Monday I can't even remember what we did. I could spend all day in Julia's bed and never want to leave. Her blankets and quilts were always so soft and smelled so good, because she dried them outside in the sun. Sometimes I'd hold them up to my face and breathe through them like an oxygen mask.

Cecily knew right away that something was going on. She didn't mention anything, but she definitely started acting differently. She wasn't quite as violent with me, and whenever Julia walked by the pool, all Cecily's friends would start giggling like crazy.

With Houston there wasn't too much to say because we had basically already talked about it. I already knew he was rooting for me. He did congratulate me at our reading lesson later that week. And our practice text that day turned out to be a gift certificate for Julia and me: dinner for two at a restaurant in the city. Houston said it was a great place for a date. And he said we should all go out sometime together, when his girlfriend came to visit from Chicago.

Julia's mother started acting differently towards me. Cecily told her or she figured it out on her own, because she came right up to me one day at the pool, wearing this tiny bright red leather coat. "So tell me, Joe," she said. "What are your intentions with my daughter?"

I had no idea that she even knew my name, and I definitely wasn't ready for this question, but I realized pretty quickly that Julia's mother never really cared if you answered her or not.

"I'm just going to do the best I can," I said.

"You're so cute," she said. "You're just like a baby. You have no idea what you're getting into. Do you like Chinese food?"

"Absolutely." I didn't even think about it. I just lied right away.

"I'd love to take you out and size you up a little. Maybe tell you a few stories."

I said that sounded like a fine idea, but I didn't think she was serious, so I forgot about the invitation pretty quickly.

I don't think Julia's dad ever knew I was in love with his daughter, or at least he didn't say anything if he did. And I never got to meet Mr. Manning face-to-face, so I have no idea if anyone had told him. But it was around this time that I figured out why he and Houston were bothering to feed those wild turkeys all this time.

I'd snuck up to Julia's room one night, and I was ironing my suit in her kitchen while she slept in the bedroom. It was quiet enough that I could hear their cars rolling on the gravel all the way from the third floor. I went to the window and watched Houston and Mr. Manning park their cars. As they walked across the lawn together toward the trees, I saw that Mr. Manning had the little suitcase this time. One of them always brought it and the other always left with it. Houston had a feedbag, and also carried a big stick over his shoulder. When they got to the edge of the woods he shook the feedbag for a few minutes, until the first turkey came out of the woods. Houston took some food from the bag. The turkey came to him and gobbled everything out of his hand. When Houston handed Mr. Manning the stick, I saw that it was a rifle. Mr. Manning cocked the rifle and shot the turkey in the face. "We'll eat turkey tomorrow," he said.

All this time I was still talking to Alvin pretty often. He didn't stop by much at the hotel, and he wouldn't come if anybody else was around, so I'd usually see him at night, on the highway. The closest McDonald's was about three miles from the hotel, and I liked to walk there for a midnight snack after Julia went to sleep. Alvin would sometimes appear and walk with me for a little while, or we'd lie on a boulder and look at the stars. He didn't bring up Julia much, because he knew I didn't like it, so we usually talked about the old days in Los Angeles. Even as he kept on getting younger and more childish, you could still tell that he'd been eighteen when he died from the way he'd act sometimes and the things he could still remember if he tried. He had a way of being two ages at once, and you could sort of talk to them both at the same time. He seemed to be doing okay, but he always seemed sleepy; and each time he came to visit me, he left a little sooner.

All together Julia and I were officially in love for about a month I guess. I never got tired of saying it or hearing it.

I learned that kissing a girl is the best way to wake up every morning. Sometimes when we kissed we pretended that we were two astronauts lost on a spaceship together or a pair of fighter pilots stranded on a desert island. Or that I was a DJ in a radio station, and Julia was such a fan that she came down to the station just to personally kiss me. For all I know there are probably a thousand kinds of love, but that one really felt like I had stolen something that I shouldn't be allowed to keep. Living with Julia, working at the hotel, playing basketball with Houston, learning to eat and swim and read, talking to Alvin and remembering his life—those months in Tennessee were basically the best months of my life. When I lived with Marcus in Los Angeles, I had sometimes wished time would pass faster, but in Tennessee I wished every day would go by more slowly. Being in love can be like that, sometimes. You are happy when normally you would be bored, and you start to forget everything else that ever happened to you.

CHAPTER SIX

Eventually it started to get colder, and every day a few more leaves would blow into the pool. I was scooping out a leaf one morning when Julia's mother pulled up to the hotel in this black convertible I'd never seen before. She honked the horn until I realized she was honking it at me. Then she waved me over to the parking lot. I remember these bright red tights she had on, and her shiny white fur coat, and how she'd put some new orange streaks in her hair since the last time I'd seen her. Right away she started talking to me in this very casual way, as if we were already good friends.

"Hope you're hungry," she said. "I've been craving Chinese all morning."

I stood there just smiling at her for a second, until I remembered that she'd offered to take me out to lunch the week before. At the time I didn't think she was serious and so I'd forgotten about it pretty quickly, but now it was actually happening. I didn't feel ready for this at all.

"Of course I'm hungry," I said. "I'll just let Julia know I'm leaving."

I went into the lobby and told Julia what was going on. She seemed even more nervous than I was.

"I should have seen this coming," she said. "My mom just can't mind her own business."

"What should I talk about? I don't even know what to call her."

"Call her Ms. Delancey. She won't answer to the name Manning anymore."

"Why don't you come?"

"I can't. That's probably why she came today, because she knows Mondays I have lunch with Granddad. And that's why she sprang it on us this way, so I wouldn't have time to reschedule."

"I'll have to eat Chinese food."

"You can still back out, you know. Just go out there and say you might be coming down with something. That'll scare the crap out of her. She won't go near you for six weeks."

"Are you nervous?"

"Why?"

"I won't go if you don't want me to."

"No. It's fine." Julia took a deep breath. "I can't act crazy just because she does. Just promise you won't remember anything she tells you."

"Okay."

"My mom has a lot of wild ideas, and she'll probably try to tell you a bunch of really confusing lies. But you won't pay attention to her, will you, Joe?"

"I never pay too much attention."

"That's what I'm counting on. Tonight you'll tell me all about it."

"I love you."

"I love you too."

Julia buttoned the jacket of my suit and kissed me, and then I went back outside and got into Ms. Delancey's car. Right away she asked me to put up the top because she wanted to play me some music. By the time I got my seat belt on, we were listening to this very bouncy country song. As we were pulling out of the woods onto the main road, she asked me what I thought of it.

"I think it sounds pretty good."

"That's nice of you," she said. "You're probably just being polite."

I had no idea what she wanted to me to say. "It really sounds like music."

"Don't you realize who's singing?"

Luckily she wasn't expecting an answer to this impossible question. She fished under her seat and pulled out this plastic double-sized CD case. On the cover was a young, sort of trampy-looking woman, about to kiss a microphone. I remember that Ms. Delancey's hands were shaking as she handed me the case.

"My stage name was Marilyn Starr." She sighed. "It seemed so clever at the time."

I finally put everything together and took another look at the CD cover. Her hair and her lips and her face all looked totally different, but you could still see that it was Ms. Delancey, maybe twenty years ago. Now that I knew she'd sung the music we were listening to, I tried to hear it better. I thought the song was too fast and there were too many instruments, but I think her voice sounded okay. I wouldn't have been surprised to hear it on the radio, although I probably would have turned it off.

"I like it," I said.

"The music business is too risky," she said. "You can spend your whole life waiting for your break, and it still might never come. Almost everybody gives up. I gave up the day I realized I'd taken a job singing at a funeral. That was the last straw for me. And the very next day I met Bill."

She turned up the music and was quiet for the rest of the ride. The bouncy song ended and a much slower one came on. It was this really sad song about a girl who loves her boyfriend even though he lies to her and smacks her all day long. About halfway through, Ms. Delancey started to sing along as she drove. She looked pretty funny, with her face all screwed up, with one hand sort of pushing into her belly, and the other on the steering wheel. Some verses she sang with her eyes closed, and so the whole performance was extremely dangerous for both of us, but the sound that came out of her mouth was actually really beautiful to listen to, and I almost started to cry. It sounded so much better than that CD, so much softer and clearer, and I remember thinking that she never should have given up, because she'd only needed some more time.

It took us six or seven songs to get to the restaurant. It was this very fancy Chinese place, with beautiful purple walls and perfect air conditioning. We ate at a booth with two glowing lanterns on the table. I was regularly eating about half of the McDonald's menu by this time, but I still didn't stand a chance in a restaurant like this. I tried to pick the foods that seemed the least disgusting, but Ms. Delancey was constantly suggesting things and offering things from her plate, so I had to eat a lot of things I knew I'd hate. That was one of the most difficult times of my life, eating that Chinese food. I choked down the little spring rolls, and this really smelly soup, and all these little nasty peppers, and rice full of disgusting pork, and my mouth felt all slippery and gross, and it didn't help that Julia's mother was chirping the whole time about how delicious it all was and dumping more nasty things onto my plate constantly, but I was a champion and ate it all. I ate it all for love.

Ms. Delancey seemed like a teenager in a lot of ways, and not just in her clothes and how her hair was cut. She actually reminded of me of Cecily and her friends. When I was around her, I always had a feeling something was about to get broken. At one point she knocked a whole tray of food on the floor—and when the waiter came to clean it up, she somehow got everybody to act like it was his fault. But I still basically liked her. I liked that she was interested in me, and I loved her clothes and how gorgeous she was, and I could almost imagine that I was eating in a Chinese restaurant with Julia in twenty years.

Once we were finished eating, she asked me, "How would you like to see Golden Oaks?"

"What's that?"

"Doesn't she tell you anything? That's the name of the house Julia grew up in. I'll give you the whole tour."

I felt like I didn't really have a choice. It turned out to mean almost another hour of driving by all these huge fields and farmhouses, and then a few miles of woods, and we had listened to Ms. Delancey's entire double-CD by the time we turned off the road. Then we drove across a wooden bridge, and crossed a little creek, and she told me to get out and un-chain this big, rusty gate. The house was on top of a hill, so we had to drive up this long, narrow dirt driveway that was starting to turn back into a forest. Then we came around a bend and slapped through some branches growing over the road; and right away I recognized the huge wooden mansion from all the pictures I'd seen in Julia's room. It turned out to be even bigger than I thought and much older too. Nothing had been painted recently, and the wood was rotting in some places, and the lawns were all crappy and ruined. Nobody was taking care of anything.

Ms. Delancey turned off the car and said, "I've got a cramp in my calf from driving. Will you rub it a little bit, Joe?" She rolled down her tights and threw her leg into my lap. I rubbed out the cramp as well as I could, and then she laughed; and we got out of the car and went inside Golden Oaks.

It was the biggest house I'd ever personally been inside. For a second—right when I walked in—I got a feeling it would be impossible to breathe in there. It turned out that I could breathe just fine, but I still knew something smelled strange in there, and later I realized what it was.

"This place was really much too big for us," said Ms. Delancey. "At least, it seemed that way until Houston came along. Then it seemed too small."

The ceilings were incredibly high. There weren't any rugs, or clothes, or telephones, or any other sign that some-body was living there. Ms. Delancey showed me the rooms where Julia and Cecily and Houston had grown up, but they were all empty now, except for some old broken furniture. There were at least two enormous curving staircases in that place, and I saw the huge master bedroom, and the parlor, the kitchen, the lounge, the den, the playroom, and the pantries and the galleys and the rooms where the servants slept a hundred years ago. I saw where Julia slipped and broke her leg, the room where the dog had her babies, the nook where they kept the computer, and rooms with names I'd never heard before.

We stopped in the room where Mr. Manning's grandmother used to make her own clothing. Ms. Delancey sat down at this big wooden loom and showed me how to use it, weaving some imaginary fabric. Then she asked me, "How old do you think I am, Joe?"

I knew I couldn't guess too high, but it didn't matter, because she wasn't waiting for my answer. "I'm forty-five years old. But I'm often mistaken for thirty-five. Were you going to guess thirty-five?"

"I think so."

"Do you know what I do all day?"

"No."

"I sue my ex-husband. I've been suing him now for a year. It's by far the easiest job I ever had." She giggled and then stopped. "Aren't you going to ask me why we're getting divorced?"

"If you want me to."

"Sometimes I wonder, if Bill and I met again tomorrow for the first time, would we fall in love again?" She jumped up from the loom and went over to sit on this black couch in the corner. When she sat down, I remember that a little puff of smoke rose up into the air. "When I first met him I fell in love with him immediately. On our very first date, I saw him save a man's life. There was an Italian tourist choking on a steak bone, and Bill ran over and squeezed him from behind and jarred it loose. I'd never seen anything like that before—but it wasn't the first, or the second, or even the third time he'd saved somebody's life that way. Before I met Bill, I used to think a person could choose to have an interesting life, but now I think some people are just born into the thick of things. Don't you want to sit down?"

"Okay."

When I went over and sat next to her, I realized the sofa was all covered in black dust. It got all over my hands and on my clothes. Ms. Delancey paid no attention to the dust, but once in a while she touched my knee while she was talking.

"On our third date, Bill took me fishing on Porcupine Lake, and I caught a nice little trout. While he was showing me how to clean it, he mentioned that he'd be in jail for the next few weeks. He said it was a misunderstanding with the IRS—but it was a pretty halfhearted lie, and he'd obviously been to jail before, and so I understood that I was falling in love with a criminal. Did you know he was a criminal?"

"I'd heard it before."

"And you don't care?"

"I've never even met him."

"I didn't care. I was young. I loved him. I thought he would clean up his act once we had enough money. That was my mistake. I thought he did it because he needed to. But he does it because he can't stop, no matter how much money he makes, and that wears on a woman after a while. Finally I couldn't take it anymore." I remember that her face was calm, but that her shoulders were all tensed up into this little angry shrug. She didn't look like Julia anymore. "After the divorce, every single one of our friends took his side. They all think I've gone insane. And maybe I have gone a little bit insane. Sometimes I call the phone company and talk to the computerized receptionists. They'll talk to you all day. But now I've embarrassed myself. You've got to tell me something embarrassing too."

It took me a while to think of anything. "I used to think my teachers lived at my school," I said finally. "I thought they slept there and waited for us to arrive in the morning."

"He's brainwashed my children against me."

"What?"

"They hate me."

"Julia doesn't hate you."

"How would you know?"

"I just think she would have mentioned it."

"I'm insanely jealous of her."

"Why?"

"Don't act so shocked. She's beautiful and charming, and everyone that meets her falls in love with her. That would make any woman jealous."

"Well, I still don't think she hates you. And Houston certainly doesn't."

"Are you kidding? Houston is the biggest lock of all. He's always hated me. From the minute Bill adopted him."

"I'd know if he hated you."

"Why? Because he's your friend?"

"That's right."

She laughed out loud, but there wasn't anything happy about the way she did it.

"He definitely cares about you. But he's not your friend. Oh my God. Am I really telling you this? I promised my therapist I wouldn't. But I promised myself I would tell you, for your own good. No, I won't tell you. It's none of my business. I'll only recommend that you be careful with him. Just look what happened to her last boyfriend."

This conversation was starting to put me on tilt, and I wanted to get out of there. I didn't want to hear any more of her stories. It was starting to seem difficult to breathe again, and my eyes were starting to itch.

"What about him?"

"Houston practically ran him out of town. I heard that right after he fired him, he threw all his clothes out into the street."

"Houston thought he was a bad influence on her," I said. "He was probably right."

"And you're a good influence?"

"He thinks I am."

"Are you on drugs, Joe?"

"No."

"I hope I didn't offend you by asking. It's just that sometimes I wonder if you're stoned. Am I really going to say this? Here I go." She took a deep breath. "Houston has always been in love with Julia."

It took a minute for me to make sure that I understood what she was saying. "He's her brother."

"I didn't realize until he was fifteen or so, when I found some of his notebooks hidden in his bedroom wall. Poor thing. I watched him try to fall for other women. He could make it last a month, sometimes a year, before he found some reason to be unsatisfied with them. A woman can live up to a man's ideal, but not if that ideal is another woman. Now he pretends to have a girlfriend in Chicago, just to keep things simple."

She stood up and went back over to the loom and started working the pedals. She gave me this little smile, like she was proud that she'd made me too confused to speak.

"It was always interesting to see how he'd react to Julia's boyfriends. If he felt threatened he would plot against them, find some way to poison her interest. It was never very difficult, because Julia always looked up to Houston. But if he saw that her new boyfriend was just a stupid crush and wouldn't last, then he'd stoke the fire, tell Julia that he approved, and try to make it last as long as possible. His favorite was a Swedish exchange student she went out with. Houston would drive them to the movies and take them out on dates, because everybody knew they couldn't last. But Alvin was a different story. Alvin scared him."

I knew I wasn't supposed to be listening to her. Julia had warned me that her mother would try to give me a lot of strange and terrible ideas, and I could tell that's what was happening right then. But it was impossible not to hear her voice.

"Alvin was a legitimate threat to take Julia away. He was making Julia question her own father. She was talking about leaving Tennessee."

"Julia said I shouldn't listen to you."

"You don't have to believe me."

"You're saying he wants to marry her?"

"No, not yet. He probably doesn't want to make a move while Bill is still around, but I'm not sure how long he can afford to wait. He's risking a lot even letting her go to college. Plenty of girls still find their husbands in college."

"I don't believe you."

"You don't have to," she said. "Just ask yourself some-time why Houston is so nice to you. Personally I've never trusted anything about him. When a boy keeps a secret his whole life, the secret eventually covers him completely, until nothing about the boy is true. Don't you wonder why he's putting on these absurd formal airs all the time? Why he talks like a middle-aged man? He found a way to act where he could be around Julia without exploding. The real Houston we never got to see."

Sometimes everything is so complicated that you just want to cover your eyes and pretend it's not there. I felt ex-hausted and confused, like I was trying to solve one of Al-vin's damn puzzles. Julia's mother had put me on this very bad and worried tilt, and suddenly I badly needed to go out-side.

"Thanks for showing me the house," I said.

She nodded and stood up from the loom. Then she came over to the couch, leaned down, and kissed me on the fore-head.

"You're not listening. It's fine. It's better for you. I prob-ably wouldn't tell you if I thought you could understand me. But now that the tour is finished, there's one more thing I've been dying to ask you. Did you even notice this whole house is burnt to a crisp?"

"Of course."

"Of course you did." She winked, like she knew I was lying. "For some reason I didn't think you had."

I don't know how I didn't notice, because looking around now it was totally obvious. Some of the walls were basically just big lumps of charcoal, and there were little piles of black soot in all the corners. I saw that the loom was all charred, and noticed our footprints in the black dust on the floor. I understood why I'd been having so much trouble breathing. I realized it had been a cloud of soot that rose up from the couch. Ms. Delancey was sort of smirking as she watched me figure all this out. "It was something in the wiring. I don't really understand these things. But nobody was here, and the fire trucks didn't arrive for hours, and everything was destroyed. Did Julia really tell you none of this?"

"Of course she did."

"You're fibbing. And that's fine. But don't you ever wonder why she doesn't tell you anything?"

On our way out of the room she stopped in the doorway to flip a light switch on the wall, but nothing happened because there was no bulb in the ceiling and all the wiring in the house had melted. "Oh, Joe, this is my dressing room," she said. "This is where I used to get dressed."

Ms. Delancey drove twice as fast on the way back from Golden Oaks, weaving in and out of traffic, singing along to her CD—and she seemed to have basically forgotten I was there, because she didn't try to talk to me again until she dropped me off at the hotel.

"I'd keep this to yourself if I were you," she said as I was getting out of the car. "You'll be tempted to talk about it, but it won't work out well for you."

"Okay, I promise." I already knew I wouldn't keep that promise. I would look for Julia as soon as her mother drove away, that very instant, and I would tell her everything. "Thanks for lunch, and I'll be seeing you around, I guess."

"Probably not for long. Good-bye, though. And good luck."

Julia wasn't home. I found out she had already finished lunch with Granddad, and now she was at a training session in the city, and she might stay for dinner. I found Cecily out by the pool, lying on her back next to the water.

"Cecily," I said. "Can I ask you a couple of things?"

"Wait."

She sat up quickly, grunting. I realized she was doing sit-ups, and I tried to stay calm while she finished them off. Then she rolled slowly over the edge of the pool and splashed into the water. She stayed under a long time and finally came up shaking her hair like a sprinkler.

"Okay, now you can speak."

"I talked to your mom."

"Hold on, I think I lost my hair band." She disappeared underwater for another minute, and then came up. "Maybe I never had it on. What were you saying?"

"Your mom took me out to lunch. Then she showed me your old house. Then she started talking about Houston."

"Wait, she asked you out to lunch?"

"Just the two of us."

"Did she pay?"

"Yes."

Cecily started to climb out of the pool excitedly. "That means she's in a good mood. If I get over there right now, maybe she'll pay for my trip to Montreal."

Now she was all in a rush, pulling on her shoes and wrapping a towel around herself. As she sprinted out the gate, she yelled over her shoulder at me, "Don't worry, Joe! Whatever the problem is, I'm sure there's nothing you can do!"

When Cecily was gone I put her towel in the laundry bin and reorganized the equipment shed about fifteen times. Then I watched TV in Julia's room while I waited for her to come home. By the time she finally walked in, it was pretty late and I'd forgotten half the things I wanted to ask her—and also how I'd planned to bring them up. She went straight to the bathroom and took this incredibly long shower. Afterward she was too tired to play poker or ask me about my day. We were lying around watching this bank-robber movie when I finally mentioned that I'd seen the house she grew up in.

"My mom took you to Golden Oaks?"

"She gave me the whole tour."

"Why?"

"She thought I might like to see it."

"So, what'd you think?"

"I never knew your house burned down."

"I guess it's not my favorite subject. Did you notice all her plastic surgery?"

"No."

"Look a little closer next time, and you'll see."

"We talked about your family too."

"Well, whatever she said, I'm sure it isn't true."

"She told me about Houston."

"What about him?"

"She told me Houston is in love with you."

"No. Don't say that."

"But that's what she said."

Julia jumped up and snapped on the light. It was too bright to open my eyes all the way. "I told you not to listen to her," she said. "She's so horrible. All she ever wants to do is stir up trouble."

"Is it true?"

"It's totally ridiculous."

"That's what I said."

"So why are you upset? What is this? Why are you confronting me like this?"

"I'm just telling you what she said."

"Well, it doesn't feel that way."

"That's not all she told me."

"I don't care what else she said. I don't have the energy for this right now. If she upset you then it's your fault for listening to her. It's hard enough for me, having a mother who hates me."

Julia jumped up and stomped off to the bathroom. Life is so full of impossible things that I can't understand. Sometimes being in love means that a girl is furious with you and you have no idea why. When she came back she was calm again but acting very young. She got herself under the covers with her arms full of stuffed animals.

"Cuddle with me," she said.

"No, I don't feel like cuddling."

"Come on. Don't make me cuddle with myself."

She opened up the covers to make room and tried to pull me in, but I wriggled away from her and rolled off the bed onto the floor. I guess I was just going to sleep there all night. I really have no idea what my plan was. After a few minutes I thought maybe Julia had gone to sleep, but then she started talking.

"Okay, fine. Let's talk about my mom," she said. "If she told you so much, did she tell you how our house burned down?"

"Something about the wires."

"Funny she didn't get more into it." Julia's voice was

very calm and quiet. "Go ahead, Joe. Ask me how our house burned down."

"No. I don't feel like asking."

"We were all in the dining room, eating dinner. Did she show you the dining room?"

"I saw it."

"We heard a knock on the door, and it was the police coming to arrest my dad. It was obviously serious this time, but my mom tried to keep on eating like everything was normal, asking for the spinach, making Houston finish this really boring story. But I could see it gradually sink in that the ride was over. He'd given her this exciting life, but now her reputation would be ruined, and every party would be different and there was nothing she could do. And she wouldn't be able to pretend that he was someone else anymore because everybody could see him."

I pushed myself onto my knees and then slowly stood up. Julia was curled up on her side holding her knees and staring at the wall on the other end of the room. I couldn't see her face.

"She always acts like he betrayed us. Like she didn't know he was a crook when she married him. She sent us all off on vacation in Los Angeles, where her sister lived, and that's where I met Alvin, on my last day there. While we were gone, Golden Oaks burned down one night. My mom was out to dinner in the city when the fire started. The insurance covered it as an electrical fire—and some days I want to believe it, because I think that house probably wanted to burn down. But most days I know I'm kidding myself. That house meant a lot to Dad's family, so I guess she figured that was the cruelest way to hurt him."

I got up off the floor and lay down carefully next to Julia. She rolled over and put her hand on my chest.

"I just want you to think about what kind of woman you're dealing with. She turned on all of us. Especially Houston. She's just looking to make trouble for everyone."

"I didn't know all that."

"Besides, the whole thing is ridiculous. Houston likes you."

"She thinks he's only nice to me because everyone knows we won't last."

"Amazing," said Julia. "She really is uncanny. She can always find the nastiest and cruelest thing to say."

"So it's not true?"

"Is what not true?"

"What everybody thinks."

"Oh, please. Don't ask me that."

"Why not?"

"Honestly? Because it makes you seem a little insecure. She's like a wrecking ball. What else did she say?"

"I can't remember."

"And you really didn't notice her plastic surgery?"

"I guess I'll try to look next time."

"I'm so tired, Joe. Can we talk about this tomorrow and just be flop-heads for a minute please?"

She still hadn't answered my question, but I couldn't ask her again now. She dozed on my chest a little, and then rolled over to finish falling asleep. An hour later I was still on my back—wide awake—watching the fluorescent stars on the ceiling very, very slowly lose their glow, when Julia started talking and moving around. It took me longer than normal to calm her down about breakfast the next day. But once she stopped destroying all the covers with her arms and legs, she finally answered my question.

"Of course nobody thinks it could last," she said. "We can't stay silly forever, and there are too many things I'd never try to talk about with you. When I go to college it'll just be a matter of time."

"Maybe so." I knew she wouldn't hear me, but I didn't care. "But we could still try."

"I warned you not to fall in love with me."

She was sitting perfectly still with her back straight up against the wall, and her eyes were wide open and shining a little. She was still breathing pretty hard from all her thrashing around earlier.

"You might always change your mind," I said. "It's possible."

"Your brother is dead and you're just sitting there. It's

so obvious who killed him, and you haven't done a thing. Don't you miss your brother, Joe?"

This was the first time Julia had ever asked me a question in her sleep that wasn't about breakfast.

"I still talk to him almost every day," I said. "He keeps getting younger and younger."

"I know why Alvin is dead, but only when I'm asleep. When I'm awake I only know it in a lot of tiny pieces, never all at once. But if I went back carefully and put together all the things I know, then it would be perfectly clear."

"Just tell me what to do."

"A girl can feel when a boy watches her that way her entire life. But it's not something that I could ever think when I'm awake. Nobody could stand to know everything they could figure out. You have to just pick a few things. Otherwise it's just too much. But you're Alvin's brother. You should be able to see it too."

"I'll do anything you want. Just tell me."

"Who's going to make breakfast?"

"I could still surprise you."

"I don't have enough money for breakfast!" Her legs were starting to move again. "But there's got to be something to eat in the morning."

She was climbing her imaginary ladder again, faster than before. I started to worry she might scratch out her eyes or something, so I tried to keep her arms underneath the blankets while I calmed her down.

"Don't worry about breakfast. I'm going to take care of it."

"How do you know there'll be enough?"

"I'll pour some cereal and make some eggs. I'll give everyone some orange juice. There'll be plenty of breakfast for everyone. Go to sleep, Julia."

Finally I got her to relax. Her breathing slowed, and I stroked the sides of her arms until she closed her eyes and started to sleep normally again. She still had on this little wrinkly frown, so I stayed there in bed with her until it finally went away, and then I got up and went into the little kitchenette, because I knew I wouldn't sleep now. I set out plates and bowls for us and opened a new cereal box, and then I got out all the eggs and lined them up next to the stove.

I knew that it was time for me to think about what I was going to do next, but it didn't come easily to me. I sat down at the table and counted as high as I could, as high as a few hundred maybe—and when that didn't work I lay down on the floor. I made myself remember the whole day: the horrible food, that big old charred house, that puff of smoke rising off the sofa cushion, Ms. Delancey's singing, and everything she'd said. When I felt my body warming up the big floor tiles, I decided to call Marcus. It was all I could think of to do.

I hadn't used my cell phone since I realized that Alvin

was never going to call it, so first I had to charge it for a little while. Once I turned it on, I saw that I already had a message from Marcus. Once I got it playing, it was nice to hear his voice again, though he sounded pretty upset.

"I don't know how to reach you, Joe, and I have no idea where you are. But I'm afraid I have terrible news."

He sounded like he was calling from the street. I could hear traffic behind him, but I couldn't tell if he was driving or walking.

"Alvin's body was found by some campers in the desert about an hour outside of Los Angeles. He'd been shot twice in the head. I can only assume it was some terrible drug deal gone bad. I thought you should know as soon as possible."

I had already known that Alvin was dead but hearing it from Marcus still felt strange, and suddenly I wished I'd left my phone on, so I could have been there when he called.

"I thought of having a funeral, but I didn't know if you would even come, and certainly nobody else would. So I'm going to have him cremated, and maybe we'll throw his ashes in the ocean. Didn't Alvin always like the ocean? I'm taking care of it tomorrow because I'm leaving Los Angeles on Saturday. I got an offer to play semi-pro basketball in China, while I get a master's at Peking University in Beijing. Pure fluency in any language can only be achieved by total immersion. Good-bye, Joe. I don't care if you contact me, but you know you always can."

There was another message from Marcus, but when I tried to listen to it I accidentally deleted them both. Then I tried to call him, just in case for some reason he hadn't left yet, but the number had been disconnected. I put my phone away, and realized I was starving. I found this old piece of pizza in the refrigerator, but it didn't fill me up. So I decided to walk to McDonald's to see if they'd let me order at the drive-through on foot. I took a peek into the bedroom to make sure Julia was still sleeping, and then went out as quietly as I could.

I was shuffling along in the shoulder about a mile down the road with fields of boulders on both sides, chewing on some grass I'd pulled out of the ground, when I found Alvin. He was lying on a boulder, looking up at the stars. By this time, he was probably about seven years old. He always had a big wad of chewing gum in his mouth at that age, and one of his teeth was still coming in.

"It's lucky you stopped by," he said. "Welcome to the enormous rock that I am lying on."

"Hi, Alvin."

I climbed up on the boulder and lay down next to him. I remember a warm wind blowing over the rocks, and the stars were extremely bright because there were no other lights.

"What are you eating, Joe?"

"Grass."

"Give me some."

I gave him some grass and he chewed it. "That grass is extremely disgusting," he said. "Good for you, Joe. And how are we supposed to explain this midnight jaunt of yours?"

"I don't know what to do."

"About what?"

"Julia thinks it's obvious who killed you. That I should have figured it out by now."

"Well, what is she expecting? It's never been your style to try to reason through a situation."

"Your body was found in the desert, you know. With two bullets in your head."

"That's upsetting," said Alvin. "I'm not sure I needed to hear that. And she knows who it was?"

"She probably thinks it was Houston."

"What do you think?"

"I hate thinking about it."

"God bless you, Joe." Alvin laughed. "Well, it's not like I'm some expert, but I've always enjoyed puzzles. Maybe I could help you think it through."

"I don't want to think it through." I could feel myself going on tilt. "I just want you to tell me."

"I can't," said Alvin. "I'm not really here. But you're smarter than you think. You always have been. How about we play a game? Do you think you can calm down enough to answer a few questions?"

"Okay. Fine."

"Do you remember the last time you saw me?"

"Yes."

"What did we do?"

"We ate."

"Where?"

"We ate dinner in a restaurant."

"And?"

"You said you needed me to come sailing with you."

"Excellent," said Alvin. "Maybe your memory was fine all along. How was I planning to pay for all that sailing?"

"You showed me all this money."

"In?"

"A bag."

"What kind of bag?"

"A little green suitcase."

"You're performing at a tremendous level," said Alvin. "Where was my body found again?"

"Somebody dumped it in the desert."

"Let's think that scenario through one more time."

"Okay."

"Anything occurring to you?"

"Why make this into a game?"

"I'm just wondering what happened to my bag," said Alvin. "That's all I'm trying to say."

"Whoever killed you probably took it."

"I love that guess," said Alvin. "That seems extremely likely. The only alternative is that he killed me because he wanted to leave all that money behind. That would be very strange behavior."

"Come on. Just tell me."

"I'm just wondering if Houston has that bag," said Alvin. "I think it could be a very helpful fact for us to know."

"Okay, sure." It seemed pretty obvious now. "We should try to find that out."

"Have you seen it around at all?"

"Sure, I've seen it around."

"You have?" He burst out laughing. "You've seen my little green cloth suitcase around?"

"At least a few times, yeah." I knew exactly what bag he was talking about. It was one of the suitcases Houston and his father were always passing back and forth when they fed the turkeys late at night. I'd seen it but I had no idea what it meant, or why I should bother to remember it. "I've definitely noticed it before."

"And you just never made the connection."

"I guess not."

"God bless you, Joe." It was the happiest I'd seen Alvin all night. "You've definitely noticed it before, but you never made the connection. Of course you didn't. That's why I'll never get tired of you, ever. Have you noticed that Houston can barely speak Julia's name without turning red and giggling like he was being tickled?"

"I think so."

"Do you remember when she dropped the fork? What happened?"

"He caught the fork before it hit the ground."

"He must have followed me to Los Angeles," said Alvin. "When I told you to check the parking lot to see if someone was following me, did you see anyone? I believe I fell asleep before I ever got around to asking you."

"Yes, actually I did." It was all rushing back to me now. The restaurant. The doggie tied to the lamp post. The parking lot around the corner. The man in the car I'd never paid attention to, because I got distracted by those bottle caps that were sparkling in the pavement. "That must have been Houston. I forgot to tell you."

"That's okay. I knew you would. God bless you, Joe."

I still felt a little embarrassed, knowing how easy I had made it for him. The whole time Alvin and I were in the restaurant dreaming about sailing around the world, Houston was waiting in the parking lot around the corner.

"For all we know, he checked into my motel," said Alvin.

"It was almost as obvious as Julia thought it was. We could have seen it so much earlier."

"Don't feel bad. I never understood my life at all while it was going on. Only much later, when I try to remember a few things and put them all together, can I realize anything that happened to me. But I never bothered to do this when I was alive." Alvin stretched again, and this time he yawned. "Suddenly I'm so tired all the time."

"What happens now?"

"You tell me."

"Do I kill Houston now?"

Alvin didn't seem surprised I'd asked. He thought it over for a while. "I'd never ask you to kill anyone on my account. But mine isn't the only opinion that matters, is it?"

"No."

"Are you sure it's what Julia wants?"

"I know she'll take it seriously," I said.

"What makes her so important? You've been in love with girls before."

"No, I haven't."

"Should I list them for you?"

"Even if I was, Julia is different."

"Do you remember Susan Porter?"

"No."

"You were in love with her in sixth grade. You liked her so much that you tried to touch every single thing she touched. Once you followed her home and kidnapped her cat, just so you could be the one to find it."

It was starting to sound a little bit familiar. I remembered stealing some of her chewing gum out of the trash, and the outline of her bra strap under every shirt she wore, and then all at once Susan Porter came back to me. It was Alvin who suggested I kidnap that fat brown cat of hers. I kept the cat in my room for two days and tried to take care of it. Susan put up all these photocopies of it all around the neighborhood, and when I finally returned the cat, she hugged me by the mailbox near her house. I put my nose into her sweater while I hugged her, and she rubbed my back in circles for a little while. Then I forgot her for six years, but now I remembered her again, and missed her just a little bit, but not too much.

"None of those other girls count."

"Do you remember Olivia Tory?"

"Who's she?"

"The point is you don't remember her. Why do you think Julia will be any different?"

"Because I'm not going to forget her." I don't know why I got so angry, but talking with Alvin about Julia always put me on this very ugly tilt. "Sometimes I wish you wouldn't come around to talk to me anymore."

"Don't say that unless you mean it."

"Come on. Just tell me what to do."

"Don't worry so much, Joe. If you don't think too much, the answer will be obvious."

"Are you really not going to help me?"

"What do I know? I can't even figure out why I'm so tired all the time." Alvin rubbed his eyes and smiled at me.

"That suit really is fine on you. It makes me want to offer you a job with an outstanding package of benefits."

That was the first time that I'd felt sort of happy when Alvin disappeared. I finished walking to McDonald's, and ate as many cheeseburgers as I could, and came home much later than I ever had before. The hotel was totally quiet as I snuck up to Julia's room. She was still sleeping peacefully when I got back, and the covers were in good shape. So if she'd been talking in her sleep while I was gone, it must have been pretty calm. I remember that I cracked my knee really hard on the edge of the coffee table as I was coming in, because I was afraid she might wake up if I turned on the light. It was an extremely painful thing to do, but I just held my knee and hopped around silently holding it in. I guess love can be something like that too sometimes: slamming your knee on a table but not making any noise because somebody is trying to sleep. When most of the pain went away, I realized I'd broken this little teapot, which had fallen off the table when I cracked my knee. I picked up the pieces of the teapot and threw them out the window as far as I could. When I got into bed with Julia, she purred a little and woke up long enough to ask me, "How many cheeseburgers did you eat?"

"Three."

"Will you please warm me up?"

I put my arms around her and warmed her up. The next

thing I remember is waking up when the first warm bit of sunlight hit me in the morning, and I guess by then I had basically decided what I was going to do. I went over to the window and looked at the sun and made myself remember all the reasons one more time, just to be sure. Then I took a quick shower and put on my suit again. After I combed my hair and smoothed myself all down, I snuck out of Julia's room without anybody seeing me leave. Then I went down to check on the pool and to wait for the day to start.

CHAPTER SEVEN

Julia and I were in love all Tuesday, and at night we saw this pretty good travel movie at the last remaining drive-in theater in Tennessee, and we were in love on Wednesday too. The hotel was basically empty, so Julia came out by the pool for most of the afternoon, and we even swam a little bit together. By this time I was good enough at swimming that we could have a decent race.

I guess there was some kind of convention in the city, and so Houston's hotel was packed and I didn't see him again until Thursday. He stopped by in time for lunch, and we sat around trying to read the newspaper for an hour or so. When Julia came by with some tea and cookies, I watched him to see how he acted around her, but it was hard to know who to compare him with, because I'd never really spent much time around a brother and sister. I did notice that he teased her a lot about the temperature of the tea and so on, and when he toasted us with his teacup, he wasn't really smiling that hard. Also, when I held Julia's hand and kissed her right in front of him, I thought I saw him flinch a little; but for all I know, every brother in the world would flinch in that situation.

I wasn't sure exactly what I was waiting for, but I knew it when it came. After the reading lesson, we got in Houston's car and headed for the basketball courts. On the way he asked me if I could drive him to the dentist the next day, because his tooth was acting up again.

"They're going to be drilling," he said. "Now, nobody knows this about me, Joe, but I've got a little phobia when it comes to people drilling around inside my head. I start freaking out. I'm pretty embarrassed about it, actually, so please don't tell the girls, if you don't mind."

"Why is that embarrassing?"

"It seems weak to me. A man should be able to stand it. Suppose I had to pull out my own tooth some day?"

"Why would you do that?"

"What if I was stranded on a desert island? Anyway, it's just impossible for me to sit there blinking like an idiot while some guy I barely know destroys the inside of my head, so I get general anesthesia whenever they do any serious work in there. I'll be groggy after, so I'll need someone to drive me home, if you don't mind."

"What kind of car is it?"

"This one."

"It's an automatic?"

"You bet it is."

"Not a problem," I said. "That's the kind of car I drive."

We played forever that afternoon. The park didn't have any lights, so when it got dark we all pointed our cars at the court and turned on all the headlights. Houston and I played on the same team. I really thought it would feel different, now that I knew he'd killed my brother and that we both loved the same girl. But it was just as fun as ever, and we won all our games pretty easily as usual. In fact I don't think we ever lost a game in all the time we played together.

When I remember Houston, this is how I picture him, playing basketball that night in the white and yellow high beams. He's spinning into the lane, surrounded by defenders. His face is shining and his eyes are wide open. He isn't looking at me but I'm sure he knows exactly where I am. And I know the ball will be coming my way any second, so I start getting ready to shoot.

The next day Houston picked me up early and told me to get behind the wheel, so I could get used to his car. I hadn't done any driving since our trip from Los Angeles, but Houston's car turned out to be basically the same as Alvin's. I made it safely into the city without getting distracted and even parked in a pretty tough space on only a couple of tries.

The dentist's office had this tiny waiting room, with nothing to look at but pictures of the worst teeth you've ever seen. Half the room was filled up by this enormous fish tank, so there was barely any space to sit. The receptionists were both behind a big glass window. I remember Houston getting annoyed at them because he had to wait for half an hour, and how he had to crouch down and complain through the little holes in the glass.

Finally the dentist came in and took him away. They had some *Sports Illustrated* magazines in there, which I could always recognize because they were all over Marcus's apartment. I'd always wondered what Marcus liked so much about those magazines, but I was too nervous to handle any reading now. So I just looked at the pictures until I saw the dentist come into the receptionist's area to take a phone call. Then I got up and walked quickly down the hall and tried two or three empty rooms until I found the one with Houston in it.

It was exactly like the dentist's office that Marcus used to make me go to in Los Angeles, with the same mechanical chair and the little spitting cup. Houston was sleeping in his chair with his mouth hanging open. I walked over to him and looked into his mouth. The room was very clean, but the inside of Houston's mouth was very nasty—full of blood and little bits of bone—and he was breathing with a kind of gurgling sound.

I was on a very strange kind of tilt. I still wasn't completely sure what I was going to do until I put my hands around Houston's throat and started strangling him. The gurgling sound stopped, and after a few seconds he stopped breathing entirely. Then I heard the dentist in the hall, so I let go. Houston started coughing in his sleep as the dentist rushed in looking all confused.

"What's going on? Why is he coughing?"

"I don't know."

"What are you doing in here?"

"I thought Houston had my phone."

"Get out of here. You're not supposed to be in here."

I went back into the lobby and picked up my magazines again. Houston finally came out about an hour later with his mouth full of gauze, still groggy from the sleeping drugs they'd given him. We drove around downtown a little bit and then stopped for some milkshakes at this diner he loved. All through lunch he was rubbing his throat, but he didn't bring it up until we were back in the car, heading home.

"I can't understand why my throat would hurt," he said. "It's my mouth that should be hurting. Does my neck look all bruised?"

"It's hard for me to tell when I'm driving."

"So pull over."

"Right now?"

"Sure."

"Where?"

"Pull over at this bridge."

Just before the road turned into a huge concrete bridge, I pulled the car over to the shoulder and then up onto some grass. Houston turned to me with a strange smile on his face.

"Turn off the car."

"Okay."

When he rolled down the window, I could hear the river bubbling away far underneath us. Houston took the last piece of gauze out of his mouth and threw it out the window, still with the same weird smile, like he had some good news that he couldn't wait to tell me.

"I can't believe I didn't recognize you," he said.

"What?"

"I think it's time we were honest with each other, Joe. We've known each other long enough. What do you say?"

"All right."

"You're Alvin's brother, aren't you?"

"Are you going to be honest with me, too?"

"Absolutely. But you were the one he picked up at Mc-Donald's that night."

I admitted that I was.

"I've caught the resemblance a couple of times in the corner of my brain, but I never made anything of it. The kid

I saw in the parking lot that night was a shaggy-haired punk with stains all over his clothes. Really an amazing transformation."

"I cut my hair."

Houston nodded thoughtfully. He rubbed his throat and coughed a couple of times.

"I think it's a lot more than that. But now I have another question for you, Joe."

"Okay. Then maybe I'll have a question too."

"Did you come in and strangle me while I was at the dentist?"

When he saw I didn't want to answer him, he patted my arm in this really comforting way.

"Don't feel bad. The important thing is that you didn't go through with it."

"You know why I had to do it."

"I know."

"You killed Alvin."

"I know I did," said Houston. "You don't have to explain yourself to me. I get it. How could I blame you for reacting that way?"

I couldn't make any sense of Houston's attitude. He was talking about killing Alvin in such a casual way, like he was showing me the breaststroke or something.

"How could you tell?"

"The dentist mentioned that you came in for your phone.

But we're not focusing on the important point. It isn't that you strangled me. It's that something stopped you. What stopped you, Joe?"

"I don't know."

"Really?"

"The dentist came in."

"Is that really why you stopped?"

"I never killed a friend before," I said. "You're the first one I ever had."

"That sounds more like it," said Houston. "You're no dummy. You knew that strangling me wouldn't bring Alvin back to life. You knew that in my place, you'd probably have done the same thing. Most of all, you knew you had too much to lose. You're risking a lot more than our friendship here."

None of these reasons had occurred to me, but they did sound pretty true when Houston said them. I rolled down my window and let the cold air blowing through the car sort of calm me down. I could smell the trees, and I thought I could smell the river too.

"You have a great situation," he said. "You have the best possible job for somebody with no education. You're learning a lot from me, and living here is changing you, turning you into a man. Strangling me would shake everything up."

"But what about Julia?"

"I'm saying that we can get past this."

"Are you in love with her?"

Houston laughed.

"You've been talking with my mother."

"Are you?"

"That word might mean two different things to both of us."

"It sounds like you are, then."

"I'll admit it if you like. But I can't be sure it's love, because I've never felt anything else. I just can't remember any second of my life where I wasn't positive I'd marry her. But that doesn't mean I will."

"So it's true then."

"Let's just say that if this isn't love, then I'd trade love for this."

"So why did you kill Alvin and not me?"

"You're acting like it's a bad thing."

"Just tell me why."

"I like you, Joe. I don't want to kill you. Life lasts a long time, and you're not doing her any harm, like Alvin was. I'm here for the long haul, so you can have your shot." Houston smiled. "Let the best man win."

"You don't believe she's serious about me."

"Of course I don't."

"You think I'm just a phase for her."

"Of course you are. She's barely more than a kid. So are you. Everything that's happening is just a phase."

"How did you kill my brother?"

"I shot him. But it's not like I enjoyed it. Now listen, Joe—"

I put my hands around his neck and strangled him again. For a while he tried to pry my fingers off his throat, and then he started waving his hands and slapping at my legs while he made these little gurgling sounds. He obviously had something extremely important to say, and so I let him go and he sat there gasping with his head between his knees, trying to get his breath back.

"This isn't safe for me," he said. "You're too damn strong."

"I've always been damn strong."

I was glad to get a little rest, because I had pulled some kind of muscle in my neck. I took off my seat belt so it wouldn't get in the way again.

"You're going to ruin everything," he said.

"You shouldn't have killed Alvin." I was thinking about all the times we had played basketball. It would have been nice to play a little more. "You should have thought of this before you decided to kill him."

"When are you going to stop thinking like a little boy?"

Then Houston lost his breath and coughed some more until I put my hands around his throat again. He fought a little while longer, but not much. I strangled his neck until he died. Then I dragged him out of the car. I let a car pass, and then hoisted him onto my shoulders and carried him over to the bridge. I propped him up on the railing and pushed him over.

The river was pretty far down there, I guess, because it seemed like Houston fell forever—long enough to spin a couple of times on the way down—and when he hit the water I could barely hear the splash. Then he disappeared right away. I think he was too skinny to float. The river was wide and strong but also very deep, so I still don't know if Houston got carried away by the current or just sank right to the bottom.

Right after Houston disappeared into the water, I really expected him to pop up and start heading to shore with a nice strong crawl stroke, because he was the one who'd taught me how to swim. Of course that was never going to happen, because he was dead before I threw him in the river. But for some reason I sort of expected it anyway.

When Alvin died, I actually talked to him more than when he was alive. And since Houston was my first friend, I figured he'd basically still be around. I really thought he'd come visit me at least once in a while, like Alvin had, but Houston never did.

That's pretty much how I killed Houston that day in the car. I felt pretty sick afterward, and threw up for a little while into the river, leaning over the railing. Then I suddenly felt freezing cold, so I went back to the car and got Houston's jacket out of the trunk. I couldn't hear anything. Both my ears hurt like crazy. I figured I'd thrown up so hard that I'd burst my eardrums. I could still taste acid on my tongue and both my eyes were stinging as I started the car and got back on the road.

I'd never driven to the hotel alone, and I really had no idea how to get there. The road got very narrow right away with thick woods on both sides. I drove pretty well for a while, but I was basically still too far on tilt to operate a car. After a few miles I made a couple of bad mistakes and crashed into a tree. I slept for a minute or two against the steering wheel and woke up to find some deer watching me through the passenger window. Both my legs seemed to be working fine, so I got out of the car and stretched out my back while I looked at the accident. The tree that I'd hit wasn't even broken, but I'd done a terrible thing to Houston's car.

Across the road there was some kind of recreation area, and a bunch of women were sitting in a circle on the grass. I think they'd been having a picnic, but now they all stood up and started to get angry about what I'd done.

"You can't even come to the park anymore," they said.

"What on earth is happening to us?" they said.

They all lit cigarettes and scowled. I thought about apologizing for ruining their picnic, but I knew I should probably just get out of there. I left the car behind and continued down the road until this trucker pulled up next to me and asked if I needed any help. I explained that I'd ruined my car.

The trucker was pretty nice, though I don't remember much of him except his moustache and the Coke can he was always spitting into. He rode with all his windows open, so I had to zip up Houston's jacket to keep warm. He said he'd been driving for fifteen hours straight, all the way from New York. I asked him how New York was. He said it was pretty good. For a little while I remember driving through thick walls of smoke that poured out of the forest on both sides of the road. He told me the forest rangers were intentionally burning the trees, to prevent forest fires. At first I thought he was joking, but he wasn't. He explained it a couple of times, but I still couldn't understand why anyone would do that.

He dropped me off about a mile from the hotel, and I walked home from there. I found Julia on the back lawn hanging laundry on a clothesline tied across some trees. By now it was the middle of the morning.

"Smell these clothes."

She handed me a shirt. It was warm from the sun and smelled sweet, and it reminded me of her even while she was standing right there. When I took the shirt off my face I saw that she was staring at me.

"You're wearing Houston's coat," she said.

"I know."

"What happened to his car?"

"I crashed it."

"Why? Where is he?"

"He's gone."

"What are you talking about?" Julia snatched the shirt away from me. "What did you do, Joe?"

"I did what you wanted me to."

"I never asked you to do anything."

"You didn't have to."

"Joe."

She came very close and held both my shoulders, looking back and forth between my eyes.

"Did anybody see you?"

"No."

"Has anyone seen you since?"

"Maybe five people so far."

"Who?"

"These four women having a picnic. And this trucker. But he said he was going to New York. You wanted me to do it," I repeated.

"Don't say that. I don't ever want to hear you say that again. We have to get you out of here."

Soon we were doing a million things: sneaking me up-stairs, packing my book bag, clearing out my room. Within ten minutes we were fighting our way through the woods, looking for where we'd hidden Alvin's car. Once we found it and pulled off the tarp, it started on the very first try. I'd already crashed one car that day, so I was relieved that Julia wanted to drive. Soon we were rolling along the dirt road, leaving the hotel behind us.

Julia hadn't done much talking this whole time, and I also noticed that she would barely look at me. Once we were on the highway she said she'd faint unless she ate something, so we stopped for lunch at this place that was supposed to have excellent cheeseburgers. It was called Frenchie's, or Frenchman's, or France or something. Julia's family used to stop there on the weekends to drink lemonade, because it was exactly halfway to their summer farm. But she hadn't been there for years.

Outside it was barely afternoon, but inside that place it was already nighttime. You could tell that most of the air had been blowing through cigarettes all day. A lot of people were drinking and playing pool. It was hard to picture Julia's family eating there. "I'm remembering it all completely wrong," she said. Then she shoved me up against the wall and kissed me. It was the hardest kiss she'd ever given me. She whispered in my ear, "Just hold me here and don't let go."

"Okay."

"I know the waiter from high school, but I don't think he's seen me yet. It was a stupid idea to come in here."

"Should we leave?"

"Just hold me here and tell me when the coast is clear. But make sure you look in a natural way."

I looked toward the bar in a natural way. The only waiter I saw was this big blond sunburned guy. He had a haircut like you'd probably see in the army.

"What's he doing?" said Julia.

"He's just standing at the bar."

"Kiss me again."

I kissed her again. I guess this was the last time I ever kissed her. It didn't last too long, because the bartender was coming over. He said, "Julia," and touched her on the shoulder, and we had to stop kissing and talk to him. With one hand on my belly Julia whispered, "Just a minute." Then she turned around and said, "Brian," and soon the two of them were hugging.

"Julia Manning," he said. "About time you stopped by. I haven't seen you since graduation."

"I know," she said. "I'm terrible, I know. But here I am."

"How's Cecily?"

"She's fine."

"Your dad?"

"He's doing fine. And yours? How are you all doing?"

"Aw, we're doing fine."

"And your folks?"

"They'll be in later," said Brian. "They'll be pretty thrilled to see you."

"Meet my friend," said Julia. "Brian, Joe."

Brian and I shook hands. I don't know why he had to squeeze so hard. His smile was amazing, but he never stopped looking at Julia the whole time we shook hands. "I've read some pretty nasty things about your father," he said. "If you want to know, I don't believe a word of it."

"Well, thanks. Thank you, Brian." She smiled at him harder than ever.

"If you want my opinion, it's all the lawyers who should go to jail. The FBI and the damn lawyers, all of them. They just can't leave a man alone to earn a decent living. We're slow right now. I'll sit with you for a bit."

"We can't stay long."

"Just sit right there," said Brian sternly. "I'll bring us all some nachos." He squeezed Julia's hand, then went off and came back with some nachos and a bunch of sodas. Then I just sat there while they talked about a lot of people that I didn't know. They also talked about churches and golf clubs, and geometry teachers, and track and field meets, and some of the funny things that happened at their high school. I had nothing to contribute, so I just sat there drinking my soda too fast, and I eventually started to go on this very blurry kind of tilt. When I went off to pee, I got distracted by some people gambling on pool, and it took almost an hour to lose all the money I had on me plus another hundred from this ATM they had there at the bar. When I got back, Julia and

Brian were singing a song I'd never heard.

"Looks like you play a mean game of pool," said Brian.

"What are you doing?" I asked Julia.

"Just telling some old stories."

"Can we leave now?"

"I guess we should." She turned sadly to Brian. "What do we owe you?"

"No Manning will ever pay me for food," said Brian. "It's just so good to see you. And I'll let everyone know you're back in action. You have to come to my barbecue on Sunday."

"I'll try," said Julia. "Tell everyone I said hi."

By the time we were back on the road, it was late afternoon and the sky had clouded over. "There are so many people that I never make the time to see," she said. "And Brian told me such a good story about my dad."

The story was about how Brian's dad owned the storage company, and it caught fire one day, and how Mr. Manning had talked to some important friends who were able to keep the publicity from getting really bad. Brian said he'd saved the family business. He thought Mr. Manning was a great man. And talking to Brian had reminded Julia that she thought this too.

"Where are we going?" I asked her again.

"I think we just have to get you as far away as possible. Nobody at the hotel would ever help the police, but you should still be out of town for a while."

"What about you?"

"I can't run away. Don't you think it's a little suspicious if I disappear too?

"Where am I going?"

"Have you told anyone you're from Los Angeles?"

"No."

"Then why wouldn't you go back there?"

"I can't drive that far myself. Plus I have no idea how to get there."

"That's why we're heading to the bus station."

"We are?"

"You shouldn't be driving Alvin's car anyway. As soon as I drop you off, I'll have to get rid of it somehow."

"When do I come back?"

"We'll just have to see," said Julia. "We didn't exactly plan this out, did we?"

I hadn't made any specific plan, but I definitely never thought that I'd be leaving by myself. If I'd known that I would have done something completely different. But I didn't have another idea at the moment, and everything was happening so fast.

"I put some cookies in your bag," said Julia. "Will you hand me one, please?"

I got the cookies out and gave her one, and then took one myself. They were pretty great cookies. They had big chocolate chunks and sometimes a little hunk of brown sugar that never got mixed in right. Maybe I ate them so fast because I had no idea what else to do. By the time Julia finished her second cookie I had almost finished the whole bag, and when she noticed she got pretty annoyed. She wrapped up the last cookie and put it in the glove compartment. "Don't eat this one," she told me. "I'm saving it for later."

I promised, but when we stopped for gas and Julia went in to pay, I could smell that cookie melting in the glove compartment. I got out and walked around the car a little, trying to forget about the cookie while I stretched my back; but then I couldn't help it. I got back in the car and carefully unwrapped the cookie, just to lick it once—just to get another tiny little taste—and then I put it back where it belonged.

Julia came back and got behind the wheel again. We drove less than a minute before she asked me, "Did you eat that cookie, Joe?"

"No."

"I was saving that cookie. I specifically asked you not to eat it."

"I swear I didn't eat that cookie Julia."

She reached over my knees and opened the glove compartment. She took the cookie out and looked at is suspiciously. "What did you do? There's chocolate all over your chin. Did you *lick* the cookie?"

I couldn't answer. I was so ashamed.

"Joe, did you really lick this cookie?"

It was the sort of thing that normally made Julia laugh, but now she didn't laugh. For a second she squeezed the steering wheel so hard that her arms started to shake. "You unwrapped the cookie and licked it."

"Just the part that was melting."

She started twisting the wheel back and forth. We were swerving all over the road. It was extremely dangerous. Finally she slammed on the brakes and pulled over to the shoulder. I didn't have my seat belt on, so I sort of crashed against the side of the car.

"We can't keep kidding ourselves," she said.

"What's wrong?"

"I'm not going to let you go back to Los Angeles and wait and wait and then slowly realize. We both already know what's going to happen."

"I don't."

"Well, I do."

It all happened so fast. Maybe I could have stopped it if it hadn't happened so fast. She found this tissue in between the seats and wiped the chocolate off my chin. "This isn't really who I am," she said quietly. "I don't even think I can say it."

"You're breaking up with me."

"There, I made you say it. Don't you think it's probably for the best? Did you really think that we were in it for the long haul?"

"Yes."

"Well, then I'm sorry that I fooled you. My only defense is that I fooled myself too."

"But I didn't do anything wrong."

"Are you sure?"

"Houston even admitted that he killed Alvin."

"Really?"

"And plus you wanted me to do it."

"Stop saying that," said Julia. "Don't ever say that again. That's a terrible thing to say. Why would you think that?"

"How am I supposed to know?"

"This is hard enough without you saying that."

"But I love you."

"I love you too," said Julia. "I've never met anybody like you, Joe. But now I'm off to college, and I'm going to start caring about things again. And I don't want to make you have to care about anything."

"But I love you so much," I said. "And I didn't do anything wrong."

"Please. You're going to make me cry."

Julia put the car in gear again, and eased us back on the road. I knew if she cried I'd start crying too, so I didn't say anything else for the rest of the ride. I just sat there trying to remember what I'd done to make her love me in the first place so I could start doing it again, before it was too late.

The station was almost empty. The last bus to Los Angeles was leaving in half an hour. I'd lost all my money playing pool, so Julia bought me a ticket and gave me some cash for the trip. I held my book bag in my lap while we waited on a bench together for my bus. Julia took my hand. "I didn't mean for this to happen," she said. "I even said it, didn't I? Remember? I said, 'Julia, you can't be falling in love with any boys right now.'"

"Can't I just keep you until tomorrow?" I asked. "We'll just spend one more day together. Then I'll go home and I won't complain at all."

"That wouldn't help." She shook her head, and wouldn't let me see her eyes. "Does it have to be tragic? Let's try not to make this too sad, if we can help it. Here, I'll get some candy."

Life is so full of impossible things that I can't understand. The main thing I did with Julia in our last few minutes at the station was wait for her to come back with some candy. While I waited, I opened up my book bag and took out the picture I had stolen of her—the one where she was standing in front of Golden Oaks, before the place burned down. Something occurred to me the day I stole that picture, and I'd forgotten it right away, but it came back pretty easily now. It occurred to me that Julia hadn't really turned out how she seemed she would from that picture. It was like she'd taken a wrong turn somewhere—just a small one—but it was enough to make her come out a little crooked. When Julia came back with the candy and looked at the picture, I think maybe she saw the same thing, because it seemed to make her a little sad.

"That seems so long ago. Where did you get that?"

"I stole it from your room at the hotel. You want it back?"

"No, you keep it."

"Should we play poker one more time while we wait?"

"We don't have time. Your bus is almost here."

We held hands on the bench and sucked on candy for the last couple of minutes until the bus showed up. Julia gave me my ticket and walked me to the gate. Then she kissed me, but not on the lips. "I'm going to miss you," she said. "Do you realize we've known each other for over two months? We met on the first day of summer. Thanks for everything, Joe. Good-bye."

"Good-bye," I said.

I stood in line with my book bag and gave my ticket to the driver, and then I climbed onto the bus and sat there while everybody else got on. The bus was already half full, and I was starting to feel sick already because it smelled so terrible in there. Someone sat down beside me with two screaming babies. Then I thought maybe I could have stopped all this if I had said or done something different. I pushed my way off the bus and ran back through the station to the parking lot, where Julia was cleaning out the trunk of Alvin's car. She looked more beautiful than the last time I'd seen her. It was like she'd taken a shower and had a nap since she left me.

"Do you want to have lunch?" I said. "Before you drive away?"

Julia looked up at the sky, where a plane was flying overhead. She tossed her keys into the air and caught them. "I should really get going."

"Are you sure?"

"I'm supposed to have dinner with my dad."

"Is he really a criminal?"

"You know he is."

"Are you going to be a criminal too?"

Julia smiled. "We'll see."

"Will you hug me?"

"You'll miss your bus."

"But I need it."

We hugged for a while next to Alvin's car. When she pulled away, she pointed at my empty shoulder. "Where's your book bag?"

"On the bus."

"You'd better get back. It's going to leave without you."

"Please don't remember me this way."

"As what?"

"As being so sad."

Julia laughed.

"Don't worry. I promise only to remember the good times. Soon that's all you'll remember too." She rattled the keys in her hand. "Okay, I'm getting in the car now."

"Okay."

She got into the car.

"I'm driving away now. Good-bye."

"Good-bye," I said. "Good-bye, Julia."

"Good-bye, Joe."

I watched her drive away, and then went back into the station. Julia had been right that I would miss my bus. One of the other drivers told me it had left three minutes ago. I'd lost my book bag and Houston's jacket and everything. I didn't really care about any of it, except for the picture of Julia.

I spent the whole night on that bench until another bus came in the morning. I got on the last empty seat and stayed on it for two days, next to a man who was heading to California to see his family. He took the bus across the country six times every year to see some children he had there. Later he spilled boiling coffee all over my legs.

We arrived in Los Angeles in the middle of the afternoon, and I spent the last of my money on a cab to Sherman Oaks. All the apartments looked the same as ever. I eventually remembered where Marcus lived—from the purple iron fence around the swimming pool—but when I stood outside his door and heard nothing but singing inside, I still wondered if I'd come to the right place.

It was excellent singing, but it was also completely different from how Ms. Delancey sang. Ms. Delancey's singing made you want to cry, but this singing sort of made it easier to breathe. I wouldn't have minded standing there and listening to it all day long, but I knew it was probably illegal. When I rang the doorbell, the singing stopped and this girl opened the door in flip-flops. She had on this snappy orange tank top, and her black hair was all shiny and loose. As soon as I saw her I remembered Marcus didn't live here anymore. He'd gone off to play basketball in China and would never take care of me again.

The girl had a movie script in her hand. She looked at me, waiting.

"I love your singing," I said. "Are you an actress?"

She nodded and smiled. It wasn't a very friendly smile, but I can't blame her. I was just this strange person who'd knocked on her door.

"I'm Marcus's brother," I said.

"Who?"

"The guy who used to rent this place."

"Oh, Marcus. Right. And you're his brother. What was your name again?"

"Joe."

"That's right. He mentioned you. He came by and left

something for you, in case you ever stopped by. Hold on a second."

She left the door open while she disappeared into the apartment, back toward where my old bedroom used to be. I could see that all the furniture was different, and in different places. The walls were lighter too. If I didn't already know I'd lived there, I never would have recognized it. She came back with this little box, tied up with black string.

"You'll see there's a note in there too."

"Do you mind reading it for me?"

"Are you serious?"

"I'd really appreciate it. I can't read just now."

She untaped the yellow note and looked it over.

"You sure you want me to read this?"

"Please."

"It says that Marcus still hasn't forgiven you, and that you should only call if it's absolutely necessary. Otherwise he simply doesn't have the energy."

"Okay, thanks."

"And there's a phone number."

"Will you write down your number too?"

"Why?"

"I could call you sometime. I could call you on my phone. Will you at least give me your name? You've known mine for a while already."

She laughed. I'd made her laugh.

"Sheryl," she said, and then she went off and got a pen and wrote her name and number on the yellow paper next to Marcus's little note.

When she closed the door I thought, *I made her laugh.* On my way out of the building, I passed the dumpster where Marcus had thrown away all my clothes one time. Now it was filled with bags of disgusting trash and a couple of broken chairs, and this ironing board. I took off my suit jacket and threw it in the dumpster. I threw my dress shirt in there too, so I was just in a T-shirt now. I only kept my pants on because I didn't have any other pants.

I wandered down to the McDonald's on Ventura Boulevard, but Francisco wasn't there. I sort of recognized the manager from before, and I explained who I was looking for.

"We called him Pancho here," he said.

"Did he finally kiss her?"

"Kiss who?"

"Carmen. She was always cooking in the back."

"Oh, Carm?" He blushed a little. "I think he probably did. They got married and went to live with his family in San Juan. That's where Pancho's mom is from. They have a baby on the way already."

"That's such good news," I said. "I mean it really is. That's such an awesome piece of news. He must have really kissed her then."

"Listen, would you like to order something?"

"I'm going to order one cheeseburger," I said. "And one chicken sandwich."

"Anything else?"

"Just let me get some money from an ATM. I'll be right back. I can't believe he kissed her!"

I ran out of the restaurant, still excited. But when I tried to take some money from an ATM, I found out I couldn't do this anymore. I remembered that Marcus had predicted this also, that before I knew it all my money would be gone. I tried a few more times, then pressed random buttons until the machine swallowed my card.

The sun was setting as I wandered over to the park where I used to play basketball. Somebody had recently paved all the courts and repainted all the lines; and all the nets were brand new too, but nobody was there. The tennis courts and baseball fields were empty. Nobody was playing sports that afternoon. Everyone was somewhere else. The sky was empty too. I sat down on a bench next to the court, and soon Alvin came out of the trees beside the baseball fields. He was, by this time, maybe four or five years old. He had these chubby little legs, and his hair was even lighter back then, and his head had a rounder shape now. His eyes were so healthy and clear. He had some caramel smeared on his cheeks and this big red ball stuffed in his pocket.

"Do you have any more caramel?" I asked him.

He shook his head. "I'm saving my last piece until just

before dinner."

Then he took the red ball out of his pocket and sort of threw it at the ground.

"Throw this ball for me, Joe. Just throw it as far as you can."

I threw the ball onto the baseball diamond. He ran over and brought it back to me proudly. "Come on, throw it farther," he said.

"I killed Houston," I told him.

"Houston? Who's Houston?" Alvin started to laugh.

"How can you not remember?" I knew Alvin just wanted me to throw the ball again, but I had the feeling this might be my last chance to ask him. I started yelling at him, "Hello! Hello, Alvin! Where are you?! I want to talk to you!"

He stopped laughing and got himself together, and then he started acting more like the age he was when he died.

"How strange," he said. "At thirteen I was less interesting than I remembered. Now I am more interesting. But it's harder to remember things I haven't done yet."

"You ran away to Tennessee, remember? Then you came back. We were going to go sailing."

"Ah, yes," said Alvin. "It's all coming back."

"I couldn't ever do that."

"Do what?"

"Leave Julia. I don't understand how you did it."

He flickered a little bit, and held the ball out toward me.

"Come on, throw it again."

"How could you leave her?"

"Throw it."

"I want to know."

"Oh, shoot," he said. "Her tummy was so soft in the morning. But I realized that she still belonged to her family, and I didn't want to live around a bunch of gangsters all my life."

"I would," I said. "I wouldn't care, as long as they were nice to me."

"I figured that a sailing trip around the world was a place that nobody would find her. But when she didn't go for it, I realized that she never would."

"And so you came and asked me."

"That's right."

"Then why did Houston follow you?"

"I don't think he wanted to take any chances," said Alvin. "Also I'd stolen a few hundred thousand dollars from him, so he probably wanted it back."

"You stole that bag of money?"

"Of course I stole it. Where did you think I got it?"

"How should I know? Maybe you earned it."

Alvin laughed.

"God bless you, Joe. Storing dirty money was the whole point of that hotel. Did you ever wonder how they stayed in business, when there were never any guests?"

"No," I said. "I didn't."

"It actually seemed funny when I stole it," said Alvin. "I liked to imagine Houston in the basement, finding the suitcase missing, calling up old Bill Manning and sweating all over the phone. When they realized it was me, I thought they might even be amused. At the time I did not think this prank would cause my life to end in murder. But there I proved to be extremely wrong. I suppose I will have to chalk it all up to experience."

Alvin climbed up on the bench and raised his little arms dramatically above his head. "Let this serve as an important lesson to us all," he shouted. "The powerful and ruthless are not generally amused by humorous pranks of this kind." He climbed back down off the bench. "Is Julia beautiful? I know I used to think she was, but by the end I couldn't see her well enough to tell."

"She's beautiful."

"Today I jumped the wall around the kiddie playground. I'm four. Do you remember that we used to switch names at this age?"

"I think so."

Alvin stuck out his chest, and he was a four-year-old again. "Throw the ball again, Joe."

This time I threw the ball a little farther, all the way into this little clump of trees behind home plate. Alvin tore after it. It was too dark to see him racing around in the trees, but I could hear him shrieking. When he came back he was completely happy and his face was red. He was too young to get tired from running.

"That was awesome," he said. "Throw it farther."

"I can't understand what I did wrong," I said. "Nothing worked out the way it was supposed to."

"Don't worry," he said. "Losing a girl isn't the end of the world. It only changes your whole life."

"Did I already tell you I killed Houston?"

"Just throw the ball again, Joey. Throw it even farther this time."

"All right. But hug me first."

Alvin climbed up on me and put his little arms around my back. He smelled like caramels. I felt his tiny freezing body and his little heart thumping away.

"Okay," I said. "I'll throw it now."

He nodded. "Just throw it as far as you possibly can."

He gave me the ball and I threw it as hard as I could, much farther this time, far into the trees. Alvin squealed and sprinted off across the baseball diamond. Then he disappeared into the trees, and I never saw him again.

Life is so full of impossible things that I can't understand. I sat down on the bench next to the basketball court. Everything was starting to get dark. The courts were empty, and the sky was empty too. Two kids showed up with a basketball and practiced dunking in the light from the tennis courts. Neither one could jump up high enough to dunk, so they just hung on the string with their fingers. Once they tore down all the nets, they got bored and left.

I felt like playing, but I didn't have a ball.

Fall was coming soon. It was already cooler in the valley than when I'd left. I wandered over to Ventura Boulevard, where everybody was driving around beeping like crazy. I walked for maybe twenty blocks; then I sat down in the marble doorway of a bank, where some hot air was pouring out of this Chinese restaurant next door.

I still had the package Marcus had left for me, and I figured it was time to open it, since I had nothing else to do. There was a little vase in there, painted like the ocean. I guess Marcus had decided to leave me Alvin's ashes. I looked at the yellow card again—at Marcus's handwriting, and then the note the girl left me. I stared hard at her name. I tried to read it. *Sheryl.* I was sure that I really did read it, even if I was partly remembering it too.

I closed my eyes. The wind blew over me and sort of crushed me into the ground, and as I fell asleep I thought about the bus, and Marcus's apartment, and that singing I'd heard. Throwing my jacket in the dumpster. Carmen pregnant. Seeing Alvin one last time. I knew things would never be the same for me, and I also knew there was a lesson here; but I was too tired to learn it now. The air was so warm, and that day I'd done one of the very best things. I'd met a girl who was really beautiful, and then I'd made her laugh.

When I woke up, the air was cooling off because the Chinese restaurant was closing. But the street was still extremely bright and full of cars and people, children, and couples holding hands. Farther down the block, a man in this filthy canvas jacket was sitting on the sidewalk in a plastic folding chair, selling these very sparkly watches out of a briefcase on his lap. I couldn't afford to buy anything anymore, but those watches looked pretty, and so I went over to look at them.

ACKNOWLEDGMENTS

The author would like to thank Anne Heltzel, Butler and Lois Lampson, Andrew Leeds, Gideon Lewis-Krauss, Jim Rutman, Ben Schrank, and Tobias Wolff for their help and support over the years.